Other Books in This Series from Peter and Paul Lalonde

Apocalypse (Book #1)
Revelation (Book #2)
Tribulation (Book #3)

Judgment

PETER AND PAUL LALONDE

THOMAS NELSON PUBLISHERS®
Nashville

Published in Nashville, Tennessee, by Thomas Nelson, Inc.

Scripture quotations are from the following sources:

The KING JAMES VERSION of the Bible.

The REVISED STANDARD VERSION of the Bible. Copyright © 1946, 1952, 1971, 1973, by the Division of Christian Education of the National Council of the Churches of Christ in the U.S.A. Used by permission.

Library of Congress-in-Publication Data

Lalonde, Peter.
    Judgment / Peter and Paul Lalonde.
        p. cm.
    Sequel to: Tribulation.
    ISBN 0-7852-6693-3
    1. Rapture (Christian eschatology)—Fiction. 2. End of the world—Fiction. I. Lalonde, Paul, 1961– II. Title.
    PS.3562.A4147 J84 2001
    813'.54—dc21   2001030826
                                                            CIP

Printed in the United States of America

01 02 03 04 05 PHX 5 4 3 2 1

To the Cloud Ten Team.
We could not be more proud of you,
or more honored to be counted
among your friends!

Preface

A WHITE MIST ROSE UP AROUND HER, shrouding the indistinct images of her dream, giving the air an unearthly chill around her and bringing with it a sensation of utter and complete abandonment. In a small part of her consciousness she realized that she must be asleep, that everything she was feeling—all of the images and memories that flitted by her confused senses—were part of a nightmare from which she could not awaken. But even knowing that it was all unreal was not enough to dispel the haunting fear that seemed to stalk her like a dark figure through the swirling clouds of smoke. If it was all a dream, it was a dream more real than the waking world . . . and far more terrifying.

The fevered hallucinations raced across her closed eyelids, unraveling a story that was too terrible to be true . . . but too real to be a figment of her imagination. Faces and places, characters and scenes raced by in a disjointed sequence that seemed to be telling the story backward and forward at the same time. She saw it all, experiencing the whole last year of her life at triple speed, and, as if from a great distance, she could hear the sound of heavy breathing, like the panting of a trapped animal. With a fresh wave of horror she realized that the sound was coming from her own heaving chest.

It was all there, unspooling like film from a maniacal projector . . . her days as a TV personality, well groomed, poised, and confident, speaking into the unblinking eye of the camera as if she were talking to an old friend. It seemed as if a thousand years had passed since those innocent, unwary days, and the Helen Hannah she saw in her mind's eye was like a foolish child, skipping and frolicking at the very edge of a bottomless abyss. If only she had known then what the future held; if only there had been some way to warn her friends and family, to spread the word of the unfathomable evil that was about to be loosed upon the planet.

The pictures continued to tumble through her mind in a mad cavalcade. She saw the earth-shattering events unfold as if she were watching a historical documentary told in screaming headlines and on-the-spot news footage. The startling emergence of Franco Macalousso, a leader whose words themselves seemed to inspire confidence and hope in a world of violence, poverty, and despair. The image of his face, an image hung on banners, flashed across television screens, and gazing from the covers of a thousand glossy magazines, conveyed that same sense of serenity and reassurance. Macalousso's strange and mesmerizing eyes cast a spell all their own, and his soothing promises sounded softly in Helen's ears . . . the words of peace and prosperity echoing over continents and across oceans.

Memories merged with visions and visions gave way to half-glimpsed fragments of her own life. Like a helpless bystander, she witnessed once again how the whole world had been divided into those who stood with the new messiah and those who had stood against him. She relived those fearful days when the reign of Macalousso and his global organization, One Nation Earth, had slowly gained a stranglehold on every aspect of human life, from the government and business of every country to the private and personal lives of each and every individual. There was no place to run. No place to hide. A new day had dawned and with it, the complete triumph of Franco Macalousso's vision of a single planet, united behind a single man . . . holding in his hands the very keys of life and death.

Resistance at first was scattered and chaotic. Those who refused to accept the glorious vision of Macalousso's new day, who refused to accept the mark on their bodies that meant they had become part of his army of fanatically dedicated disciples—such "outlaws" were mercilessly hunted down. Those who were captured were subjected to the same indoctrination as all the rest: the same strange helmet slipped over their heads, the same powerful and persuasive technique that erased the last vestige of resistance and transformed the most determined rebel into a docile citizen of the new world. Of course, for anyone who could resist these powerful inducements, there was another remedy: death.

But slowly, painfully, one small step at a time, an organized underground had emerged. They were called Haters by Macalousso's minions and the name fit. They *were* haters—haters of the reign and rule of this seemingly benevolent and all-wise ruler who, beneath his charismatic exterior, had but a single, sinister strategy: to turn the whole world away from its Creator and toward an unholy allegiance with the forces of darkness that lusted to be worshiped in the place of God.

It had taken Helen a long time to realize what was really happening behind the facade of Macalousso's sweeping agenda for change. Even as the planet seemed to settle into a whole new era of global peace and plenty, it was clear, for those with eyes to see, that the greatest deception in the history of mankind was being perpetrated. The freedom Macalousso brought was, in reality, slavery, the liberation, the cruelest form of bondage that bound not only the body, but the soul and spirit.

And it was in the realm of the spirit that Helen, and a handful of others like her, did battle against One Nation Earth and the powers and principalities that pulled the puppet strings. Her breathing was hard and fast now, as she relived in her dream those days on the run in abandoned subway stations and old warehouses, dodging the police, always on the run, half-starved and shivering in the cold of a late-night alleyway.

Those had been hard times, but they had also been good times. In was in those days that Helen had learned to pray, to call out to God and seek His strength to see her through, day by day and sometimes, minute by minute. She had learned to read His Word, and to take to heart the promises she found there. She had, in short, discovered that the only way to survive in a world full of deadly enemies was to have faith in a Defender more powerful than any foe, more determined than any adversary. She had discovered Jesus.

As she spoke the name through parched and cracked lips, her tortured breathing began to slow. She felt calmer now, as a bright ray of hope broke through the swirling fog of her tormented dream. It had been Jesus who had walked beside her every step of the way through her long journey to becoming a freedom fighter against the forces of Macalousso. Jesus had sustained her, given her courage and resolve to keep fighting and, when those around her in the resistance faltered and fell behind, it was Jesus, speaking through her, who stirred their spirits again and gave them the strength to fight another day. They may have been Haters, but they were also lovers—lovers of God's Son who had called them to this terrible battle in a time of tribulation.

And when the day had come when she had been run to the ground, like an animal, by the elite Hater hunters of Macalousso's armies, it was Jesus who had kept her from despair, silenced her tongue when the torture was so unbearable all she wanted to do was to scream out the names of her friends and fellow rebels, if it would only stop the awful agony of the enemy's torments. Jesus had been with her then, closer than a brother, experiencing every moment of those terrifying interrogations with her, until, at last, she fainted away into blessed unconsciousness, the secrets of resistance still safely locked away between her lips. Jesus had stood with her and there was nothing they could do to her now to separate her from the love of her Savior.

Her breathing was steady now, the flickering behind her eyelids had dimmed and disappeared. She lay quietly for a moment as the vapors of the dream thinned and dispersed. *Perhaps*, she thought, hoping against hope . . . perhaps it had only been a dream after all. Perhaps Jesus had saved her from her long nightmare and when she opened her eyes she would be safe in her own bed, in her own home, back again to the way things used to be before she had ever heard the name of Franco Macalousso.

Her eyelashes fluttered and, after a moment, her pale blue eyes opened. Immediately a cry escaped her lips as a blinding white light pierced her vision. The world around her was a glaring expanse of nothingness, as barren as an ice floe in the Arctic wilderness. Wherever she was, it was certainly not safe in her bed. This was a place more alien than any she had ever known and it seemed as if her nightmare had not only become real, but more intense than even her frightened imagination could conceive.

It took a long moment for Helen's eyes to adjust to the burning brightness and when she was at last able to make out the shapes and forms around her, she heard her own breath draw in sharply. She wondered if she would ever fill her lungs again as she stared up at the gleaming blade of a guillotine poised high over her head. She tried to move away, wrenching aside to avoid the razor-sharp edge and only then discovered that she was strapped down tightly on her back, her face turned directly toward the death-dealing device. This was no longer a dream. This was real, a reality she could never shut out. One Nation Earth, the frantic months of hiding and cowering, the mark of the beast of Macalousso seared into the flesh of millions upon millions of deluded human beings: it was real . . . horribly, unalterably real.

A face suddenly swam into focus before her. The slightly sneering smile, the strange gleam in the eyes, the look of menace lurking beneath the surface of caring and concern—it was all too familiar and she stifled a sob at the thought that the last thing she would see would be the face of Franco Macalousso.

"You once told me," he said, in a voice that oozed with oily charm, "that the God you worship gives everyone the freedom to chose his own destiny. Isn't that right, Helen?"

She nodded mutely, not trusting herself to speak, lest she might betray her fear and loathing.

"Well, then," the world leader continued with an ironic smile, "I guess the time has come for you to choose."

Helen pulled at the restraints that held her down. "I already have chosen," she replied, staring up at him defiantly. "I've chosen to go home."

Macalousso reached up with his well-manicured hand, the diamond rings decorating his fingers glinting in the unearthly light, and grabbed hold of the release lever on the guillotine.

Helen closed her eyes and whispered to herself in a voice hoarse with emotion. "Yea, though I walk through the valley of the shadow of death . . . "

With a snarl Macalousso yanked down the lever and Helen could hear the faint, metallic echo of the blade as it descended toward her exposed neck. She held her breath, her eyes clenched tight, the name of Jesus trembling on her lips. The end had come . . . a new life, an endless life of joy and peace and abundance was about to begin . . .

A long moment passed. Still holding her breath, Helen opened her eyes, peering through slits up into the harsh glare of the featureless world of her captivity. Another moment passed, and still the end she had prepared herself for didn't come. She opened her eyes wider, and saw once again the leering face of Franco Macalousso hovering over her. In his hand he held the glimmering blade of the execution machine, suspending it scant inches over her neck.

"Come now, Helen," he said, his voice dripping with scorn. "You didn't really think it was going to be that easy, now did you?" His diabolical laughter rang in her ears, louder and louder until she thought she would go insane from the sheer, malevolent sound of it.

Chapter 1

THE MAN AND WOMAN sat in elegant leather chairs at the far end of the enormous office, the penthouse view of the twinkling city lights spread out beneath them from the floor-to-ceiling plate-glass windows. The room was richly appointed in hand-rubbed mahogany and brocade, sterling silver, and thick, patterned carpets. At the opposite end of the office, a desk took up nearly one entire wall. Behind it was the flat screen of a huge television monitor on which a ghostly image flickered.

The picture on the screen could not have been in sharper contrast to the plush surroundings of the executive suite. In a dingy prison cell, a lone figure knelt beside a rickety cot covered with a threadbare blanket. On the floor was the remains of a meager meal and, even as they watched, a rat scurried up and scampered away with a crust of bread. The figure turned, her profile lit by the dim light slanting through a peephole. It was Helen Hannah, her face smudged with grime, her clothes tattered and grimy, tears welling in her eyes as she prayed silently from the deepest depths of her captivity.

The man, sipping a tall drink, watched impassively, a cigarette balanced between his fingers. It was Franco Macalousso, self-proclaimed savior of planet earth, perched high above his domain in an office specially designed to inspire awe and dread in all who stepped over its threshold.

Beside him sat a tall, statuesque woman attired in an immaculately tailored blue-silk business suit. She wore an air of self-confident arrogance that clung to her like an expensive perfume and she seemed not at all intimidated to be in the presence of the most famous and revered individual in all human history. The cool green eyes of Victoria Thorne sized up Macalousso with the same cold calculation with which she measured everything. Her mind, like a steel-toothed trap, was set to evaluate all encounters by two simple criteria: what did this person want from her? And what could she get from him?

"It's good to see that one of the most dangerous leaders of the Haters is safely behind bars where she can no longer spread her poison," Victoria said, her voice perfectly pitched to express her loyalty and dedication. Her attorney's instincts told her that Macalousso was showing her this simply to get her approval. He had an agenda, of that much Victoria Thorne was sure. She reached forward and opened a gilded box of cigarettes, lighting one for herself and, inhaling deeply, sat back in the plush chair, alert and poised, like a cat ready to pounce.

"You'd think so, wouldn't you?" replied Macalousso smoothly, his voice betraying no emotion. He reached for the remote control lying on the thick glass coffee table in front on them. "And yet . . . " He flicked a button and the picture on the screen dissolved into an evening news report. The grim voice of a reporter could be heard over video footage of burning buildings, shattered windows, and bleeding bystanders being carried into waiting ambulances.

"Another Hater attack has left the city reeling with shock, fear, and anger," the anchor reported, "after a car bomb destroyed an entire wing of the downtown Riverview Hospital this evening."

The picture switched to a black-and-white mug shot of a desperate-looking young man, staring defiantly into the camera lens. "William Rawson," the reporter continued, "a self-professed ringleader of the Haters, has been detained for the crime, the fiftieth Hater attack in the city within the past three months."

Another camera angle revealed the anchorman at his desk, looking solemnly at his audience. "These deranged zealots are the only stumbling block that remains to be removed before our messiah, Franco Macalousso, can usher in his promised reign of peace and prosperity. It is the duty of every citizen of One Nation Earth to report any and all Hater activity to the proper authorities at once, regardless of who the perpetrator may be. Mother, father, brother, or sister— any enemy of Franco Macalousso is an enemy of us all."

"We may have vermin like Helen Hannah behind

bars," Macalousso said as he switched off the screen, "but the resistance continues and, I dare say, my dear Victoria, it's getting more intense. These . . . unfortunate incidents are on the rise. Something must be done. Someone must be held responsible."

There was no mistaking the implied threat in his last words. Victoria crushed out her cigarette in a carved-jade ashtray and cleared her throat. It was time to make her case. "I can assure you, Your Eminence," she began, "that the Justice Department is doing everything in its power . . . "

Macalousso waved away her excuses. "I'm afraid our brave new world is getting lazy and complacent," he interrupted. "I'm sure you can well remember a time, Victoria, when citizens would light up police switchboards with reports of Hater activity. Children would betray their parents. Neighbor turned against neighbor. My people had joined together to rid the world of this human garbage."

He spat his last words and Victoria checked her impulse to recoil from such a display of naked hate. It was a side of the messiah few people saw, a side that, once viewed, put all his promises of peace and harmony into a sinister new light. If there was anything to be learned from working in close proximity to the new ruler of a united globe, it was that he didn't like to be crossed. By anyone. For any reason.

"Perhaps," Victoria ventured, "we could deploy more troops. A house-to-house search in suspected neighborhoods. Identity checks . . . "

Once again Macalousso waved her words away with an impatient gesture. "I'm not sure you understand the gravity of the situation, Victoria," he said, his voice low and menacing. "If the Haters continue unchecked, they will in time gather more to their deluded cause. They will become martyrs, heroes. Our people will begin to wonder why they fight so hard against my rule. Why they are willing to risk everything for the dangerous beliefs they hold dear. What are now a few scattered pockets of resistance may in time grow into a full-scale rebellion. That is, unless . . . "

He paused, his eyes gleaming with an eerie light in the dim recesses of the cavernous office.

"Unless, Your Eminence . . . ?" Victoria prompted.

Macalousso smiled and she felt a chill race involuntarily down her spine.

"Unless," Macalousso continued, standing until he towered over her, his figure silhouetted dimly in the city light reflected from the windows, "we give them a good reason to hate the Haters. We've got to awaken the root of bitterness that lives in hearts of all men and women. We've got to mobilize the citizens of our new world to eradicate the last traces of rebellion against my rule."

He raised his arm high as if he were about to call down thunder and lightning. "I must have one thing, and one thing only: a world that belongs completely to me!" he spat contemptuously. "I'll have no more of these pathetic lambs of God bleating their message of forgiveness and salvation!"

He was shouting now, and his voice seemed to rattle the

windows. "I'll find them all, each and every one and destroy them utterly!"

There was a long moment as Macalousso struggled to regain his composure. He was panting as if out of breath, a fine sheen of sweat beaded his forehead, and Victoria could see a vein throbbing angrily in his neck. She waited as well until it seemed that he had gotten control over himself again and then, hoping it was safe to talk, she spoke in a voice low and conspiratorial.

"I assume Your Eminence has a strategy for achieving this end," she said, looking up at him with utter confidence. It was important to convey her total loyalty, especially now that she knew that her job at the Justice Department was hanging in the balance, as the messiah searched for a scape-goat on which to pin the crimes of the Haters. Victoria Thorne had to tread very carefully now—her position in the new world government depended upon it.

Macalousso smiled and Victoria breathed a secret sigh of relief. She could see that he had been placated . . . at least for the moment.

"I knew I could depend on you, Victoria," he purred. "You have a remarkable ability to ask the right questions at the right time."

"Thank you, Your Eminence," she said, beaming. "Just tell me what you need from me and consider it done."

"What I need?" echoed Macalousso, the smile frozen on his face. "What I need should be obvious by now. We must show the world the true nature of our enemy. Not just by arresting them and disposing of them one by one, but in a single, grand gesture—one that will prove beyond a shadow of a doubt that the Haters must be exterminated if the world is ever to know the peace that I want to bring."

The wheels in Victoria's mind spun rapidly as she tried to string together the clues Macalousso had dropped to reveal his purpose. The surveillance video of Helen Hannah . . . the news report of Hater activity . . . even the fact that she herself, the star attorney on Macalousso's hand-picked Justice Department team, had been selected to handle this case. . . it all had to mean something. And now he was asking for a grand gesture, something that would prove his case, once and for all.

With relentless logic Victoria assembled the evidence. It all added up to only one thing. "I understand," she said at last. "A precedent-setting case. A trial to end all trials, proving forever that the Haters want only destruction, while you want to bring the world together."

Macalousso beamed. "As I said, Victoria, I always knew I could depend on you. From the moment I laid eyes on you, I knew that you had special abilities, talents I could use to accomplish my ends."

He reached out and she took his hand, letting him pull her to her feet. They stood face-to-face, so close she could feel his hot breath against her ear as he leaned in to whisper. "This will be your greatest achievement, Victoria," he hissed. "The whole world will be watching as you make an example of God's own champion. You will demonstrate, though your brilliance and sheer power of persuasion, what it really means to follow this so-called King of kings. And when you're done with her—"

"Her, Your Eminence?" Victoria asked. "You mean—"

"Who else?" replied Macalousso with wicked glee. "She is their strongest advocate, the one whose faith even I have been unable to shake. Imagine the impact it will have when you bring her to her knees, begging for mercy and declaring me her lord and master!"

He was stroking her black, shiny hair now, as a father would to show approval a loyal daughter. "Your work for me in the past has been exemplary," he continued. "Your relentless pursuit of . . . justice has been unmatched. I can think of no one better to present my case for all the world to hear. And when they judge for themselves—" he slammed his clenched fist into the open palm of his other hand, "the Haters will be history!"

Victoria now found herself struggling to control her excited emotions. Ambitions surged in her blood like a drug. "We show them the truth of your kingdom," she declared.

"Against the lies of my mortal enemy," Macalousso interjected.

Victoria turned to him. "But," she said, "what about Helen Hannah? If we're really going to put her on trial, she's going to need a defense lawyer. We've got to make it look real. There can be no question that she is receiving a fair hearing."

"I agree totally," responded Macalousso. "She'll have the best lawyer money can buy. Someone who appears to all the world as your equal. Someone who is every bit as eloquent and persuasive as you are, my dear. But someone we can depend on, as well . . . to ensure the final outcome."

"No self-respecting attorney in his right mind would take the case," Victoria cautioned. "It's the kind of thing that could destroy a career. Unless . . . "

Macalousso could see the gears of her mind turning once again. "Unless what?" he prodded after a moment.

"Unless we can bring some pressure to bear," Victoria replied, and the smile she gave him was every bit as wicked and chilling as his own. "Unless we can turn some screws."

"It sounds to me as if you already have someone in mind," said the delighted Macalousso.

"Leave it to me, Your Eminence," Victoria answered. "I trust you will be very pleased with the outcome."

"For your sake, I hope so," he replied, and the look in his eye was unmistakable. There could be no mistakes made. The trial of the century . . . the trial of the millennium must unwind like clockwork.

Chapter 2

THE OFFICE OF MITCH KENDRICK was neat and tidy, equipped with all the latest communications aids and perfectly suited to take care of business. It was a mirror reflection of the personal and professional characteristics of its occupant, a thirty-five-year-old attorney, driven, ambitious, with his eyes on the prize. In short, Mitch Kendrick was a man on the move, a lawyer poised for a career-making case.

In sharp contrast to Kendrick's air of brisk efficiency and well-groomed good looks, the woman who sat across the desk from him hardly gave the appearance of possibly furthering his career. In fact, if any of his more important clients had seen him talking to the young, attractive, but decidedly disheveled young woman, they might have wondered just exactly what Mitch Kendrick was doing wasting his time on such an obvious lost cause. It was the same thought that crossed the lawyer's mind as he glanced impatiently at his watch and tried to focus on what his visitor was saying.

"I've heard that you're the only one who might be able to help," said the twenty-six-year-old woman with a desperate look in her eyes. "I had no choice but to come here, Mr. Kendrick. You've got to understand what we're up against."

Mitch cast a surreptitious look at the pale face across his desk. Dawn Blushak might very well have turned a few heads with her bright blue eyes, flawless complexion, and perfectly proportioned features framed by a head of blonde hair. But today her hair was dirty and matted, her skin was smudged with what looked like a week's worth of grime, and the pleading look in her eyes was more than a little unsettling. Mitch couldn't help feeling a little sorry for her, sorry for her plight and for the obvious fact that she was living at the very margins of existence. But feeling compassion wasn't an emotion he was familiar with and the strange sensation made him uncomfortable and nervous.

"Look," he said, trying to sound detached and businesslike, "there must be a hundred other lawyers who can handle this kind of thing for you." He leaned forward. "Frankly, Miss Blushak, I don't think you can afford me."

"But we've got money," Dawn protested as she pulled a wad of bills out of the pocket of a soiled leather jacket. "We just can't spend it. We're shut out of the system. Totally shut out."

"And whose fault is that?" Mitch shot back. "All you have to do is pledge allegiance. Join One Nation Earth. You can rejoin society, be part of the opportunity and prosperity Franco Macalousso has promised." He paused, fixing the young woman with a penetrating stare. "Why would you want to resist that? It's so simple. So easy."

"As easy as taking the mark, is that what you mean, Mr. Kendrick?" Dawn responded, her eyes flashing with anger. "All we have to do is get a little tattoo and we can buy and sell just like everyone else, is that what you mean?"

"Something like that," replied Mitch, a bit unnerved by her vehement tone.

Dawn stood up and leaned over the desk, her uncombed hair falling over her face until she angrily pushed it away. "Have you ever seen what happens to the people who take that mark?"

Mitch paused for a moment, then held up his right hand where a small symbol could be seen just above his shirt cuff. "You mean people like me?"

The two stared at each other for a long moment, until Dawn sat back down. "Mr. Kendrick," she said at last, "I'm no Hater. And neither are my friends. We don't care about Franco Macalousso and his brave new world. We just want to be left alone to live our lives. We can't even feed our-selves. If they won't let us buy food we'll starve to death."

It was Mitch's turn to sigh. As much as he wanted to be stern and cold toward the miserable creature in front of him, he couldn't overcome the feelings of pity and empathy he felt. "Look," he replied, "even if I did want to help, there's nothing I can do. You and your friends are breaking the law. It's as simple as that. Whatever you believe or don't believe, is it really worth starving to death to prove your point?"

"How much is freedom worth to you, Mr. Kendrick?" Dawn asked.

From the doorway behind them a voice suddenly interrupted, "I'd be interested in knowing the answer to that myself, Mitch."

Spinning around, Dawn and the lawyer saw the svelte, impeccably dressed figure standing at the entrance of the office.

Mitch swallowed hard. "I think you'd better leave, Miss Blushak," he said, but the young woman, who had caught a glimpse of the official One Nation Earth badge pinned to Victoria Thorne's purse, had already gathered up her grungy overcoat and scurried out a side door.

Victoria moved as if on greased ball bearings into the room and across to where Mitch stood behind his desk. "Not giving aid and comfort to the enemy, I hope," she insinuated with a silky smooth voice.

When Mitch spoke it was obvious that he was trying hard to control his rising anger. "What are you doing here, Victoria?" he demanded. "I thought getting dumped by you meant we'd never have to see each other again."

Victoria clucked her tongue, a smile playing across the glossy lips. "Is that any way to treat an old friend and lover, Mitch?" she asked, sitting down uninvited in the seat recently vacated by the desperate Dawn. "I was hoping we could get off to a fresh start."

"There's nothing to start!" Mitch shot back. "We finished it a long time ago, remember?"

"Don't be that way," she replied with a pout. "I come bearing gifts. Very substantial gifts."

"Not interested."

"Really?" said Victoria, arching her eyebrow. "Then you're not the Mitch Kendrick I once knew. That Mitch Kendrick would have jumped at an opportunity like this. That Mitch Kendrick would have recognized a once-in-a-lifetime career move when he saw it."

She watched as her words found their mark. Mitch was hooked even as he tried not to show his interest in the bait she was dangling before him. He sat down and, drumming his fingers on the table, gave her a steely look. "Okay," he commanded at last. "Let's hear it."

She smiled back and shook her head. "Not until you turn it off."

Mitch hesitated, trying to decide whether it was worth calling her bluff. Then, with a sigh, he reached across the desk and, sliding open a small hidden panel beneath the gooseneck lamp, shut off the power to a hidden recording device.

"Happy?" he said, with an edge to his voice. "Now what do you want?"

Victoria smirked. "I'd hate to think you'd betray my confidence, Mitch," she replied.

"Oh," he said bitterly, "you mean like you betrayed mine? Don't worry, Vicky. Everything I need to know about you, I've already got on file. It's under *B* for Back-stabber. Or maybe it's *B* for—"

"You brought it on yourself, Mitch," she interrupted. "I never promised you a thing. Certainly not loyalty. I thought we had an understanding, you and I. No ties. No commitments."

"Spare me the justifications, Victoria," Mitch snarled. "I'm a busy man."

"Too busy to take on the biggest case of your career, Mitch?" she responded smoothly. "Too busy to make history?"

In the silence that followed, the sound of the ticking clock was like a beating drum. "I'm listening," he said at last.

"Of course you are," replied Victoria, reaching in her purse for a cigarette. She held it between her lips, waiting until with a sigh, Mitch reached over and lit it for her.

"You're no fool," she continued. "Only a fool would turn down a chance to stand before the entire world in One Nation Earth's Supreme Court of Justice. Only a fool would spurn the opportunity to show off his talents as a top defense lawyer. Only a fool would walk away from the greatest and most important trial in human history."

"That's quiet a pitch," said Mitch, impressed in spite of himself. "Now, suppose you fill me in on the details behind that grandiose snow job."

"Ever heard," Victoria asked, "of Helen Hannah?"

"Helen Hannah?" Mitch echoed. "You mean the Hater?"

Victoria nodded, drawing deeply on her cigarette. "The very same." She leaned forward. "I have it on good authority that Helen Hannah is about to go on trial for crimes against humanity. She's a symbol, Mitch. A symbol of an entire movement that stands opposed to Franco Macalousso and his goal of complete global harmony. She needs to be made an example. She needs to be brought down before the eyes of the whole world, exposed for the rebel and terrorist that she is."

"Let me guess," Mitch interjected, "as One Nation Earth's chief prosecutor, you'll naturally be the one bringing her down."

Victoria smiled again as cigarette smoke rose up and surrounded her in a ghostly wreath. "You're one step ahead of me, Mitch. But this visit isn't about my job. It's about your job . . . and the job we'll be doing together."

Mitch blanched, his face turning pale. "You want me . . . to defend Helen Hannah?" he asked in a whisper.

"You were my first choice," she assured him. "My only choice. I've never seen a better defense attorney than you, Mitch. You can make a jury believe anything. You go as far as you have to in order to prove your point. Only this time, you won't have to go quite so far."

"What's that supposed to mean?" Mitch asked suspiciously.

"The verdict in this trial has already been decided," she countered. "It's up to you to make the world believe it's fair and unbiased."

Mitch stared at Victoria as she exhaled a long, languid trail of smoke. *How could someone so beautiful,* he thought to himself, *be so evil?*

"Why me?" he asked at last. "You've got your choice of a million competent lawyers."

Victoria laughed, a hard and chilling sound. "Think

about it, Mitch," she answered. "Your background is perfect. Your own father was a notorious Christian. That gives you more than enough motivation to play the part to perfection. Besides, you're the only attorney who has any real experience in this kind of . . . criminal activity."

Mitch shook his head. "I think one Hater trial is more than enough for any career."

It was Victoria's turned to give him a long, slow look, like a snake sizing up her next meal. "Maybe I haven't made myself clear," she said at last. "I'm not asking you to take this case. I'm telling you."

She watched with satisfaction as her words made Mitch start. Was it fear she saw on his face? Or anger? Either one gave her a delicious sense of power over Mitch Kendrick.

"You can't do that," he said at last, working hard to hide the trembling in his voice.

"I already have," was her curt reply as she stood suddenly and, dropping the cigarette butt, crushed it into the carpet beneath her spiked heel. "Ten o'clock, Mitch," she said, turning and slithering toward the door. "Judge's quarters. World Justice Building. Don't be late."

Chapter 3

THE ANTIQUE CLOCK ON THE WALL, surrounded by diplomas and framed photos of celebrities and politicians, chimed the last stroke of ten o'clock as the door opened to the chambers of Judge Thorton Wells, an austere, white-haired man with a permanent scowl and a look of intimidation long perfected from his decades in black robes. The oak-panel door swung open without a sound and Wells's equally stern secretary ushered in Victoria Thorne and Mitch Kendrick.

While the One Nation Earth Supreme Court judge and the Justice Department's top prosecutor exchanged pleasantries, Mitch took the opportunity to glance around the stately, book-lined offices. *Some lawyers,* he thought to himself, *wait their whole lives to be invited into the inner sanctum of a judge of Thorton Wells's caliber.* And here he was, at the very pinnacle of legal power. So why did he feel uneasy?

With the small talk out of the way, Victoria and Judge Wells crossed over to a large maple table at one end of the room on which were stacked two identical piles of paper.

Gesturing for Mitch to follow, Victoria stood aside as Wells picked up one pile and handed it to the defense attorney.

"It's all here," he announced brusquely, "in black and white. Learn your parts and everything will go smoothly." He glared at Mitch. "Ms. Thorne tells me you're capable of learning your part, Counselor. I trust you won't disappoint us. A great deal depends on correct procedure in this trial. I can't stress that enough."

Mitch, who had been glancing through the stack of papers, looked up, his face reflecting the growing sense of manipulation he had been feeling ever since Victoria first walked into his office. "But," he protested, "it's all been scripted. The whole trial. From my opening statement—" he flipped to the last page, "—to the verdict."

"Of course it has," fumed Wells. "I told you, we can't afford to leave anything up to chance. Isn't that right, Ms. Thorne?"

"Mr. Kendrick understands the importance of his job, Judge," she replied smoothly. "I can assure you of that."

At her words, Mitch slammed down the stack of papers, sending them skidding across the smooth surface of the table. "Now wait just one minute," he said, his voice rising. "I'm not sure I get this whole deal, but I'm sure of one thing. This whole trial is rigged, soup to nuts!" He turned to Victoria. "I guess you conveniently forgot to mention that in your little sales pitch, Vicky." Facing the judge, he continued, "Find yourself another performing monkey, Judge." He began to stride to the door.

"Where do you think you're going, young man?" Judge Wells bellowed, and the tone of his authoritarian voice stopped Mitch dead in his tracks. "Sit down and listen up," the judge continued, and Mitch found himself obeying almost without volition.

Towering over Mitch, Wells continued his tirade. "I don't know what Ms. Thorne did to get you through those doors, Kendrick," he shouted, "and frankly, I don't care! All I know is that she says you're the right man for this job and that means you will do what you're told to do, without question. Your only duty is to One Nation Earth and our messiah, Franco Macalousso. And that means that you are going to make this trial look real and sound real and feel 100-percent authentic. And if it isn't, then the next trial will be yours, Mr. Kendrick. And I can assure you, by the might of Macalousso, that the verdict will be 'Guilty as charged.' And the sentence—" He paused. "Let's just leave that up to your imagination, shall we, Mr. Kendrick?"

Mitch shot a look from the judge's florid face to the calm and composed expression on Victoria's finely chiseled features. Outside the window came the faint sounds of people chanting slogans outside. The trial was about to get under way and Mitch Kendrick had a starring role in the production.

⁘

On the street far below the judge's chambers, a crowd pressed angrily against a police barricade, their voices raised in what sounded like an animal howl of hatred and blood-lust. Standing nearby, trying hard to make herself heard above the roar of the mob, a TV news anchorwoman stared into the camera and made her report: "We're here today outside the One Nation Earth Supreme Court building on the first day of what promises to be the most important trial in the history of this planet."

Behind her, the crowd pushed against the barriers like a living organism trying to break free of its confines.

She continued, "The charge of crimes against human-ity has been leveled at one of the ringleaders of the notori-ous Haters terrorist organization, none other than the infamous Helen Hannah."

At the sound of her name, the mob let loose a shriek that sent a momentary tremor of pure fear over the face of the newswoman. It was an expression clearly seen by every viewer around the planet, including the small band of battle-hardened comrades in arms gathered around a flickering picture tube deep in the bowels of an abandoned subway station.

Their filthy, cluttered headquarters was filled with makeshift computer stations, graph charts, and maps hung from the stained and dusty walls. Two women and three men huddled together, watching the newscast. Two brothers, Jake and Tony Goss, shared the same deep-set eyes and dark curly hair. Husband and wife, J. T. and Sherri Comstock, held hands as the light from the television played across the smudged and haggard faces. An attractive black woman,

Selma Davis, kept one eye on the report and another on the entrance to their hideout, alert and vigilant as only an experienced guerilla warrior could be.

"Despite overwhelming evidence to the contrary," the reporter continued, "Helen Hannah, who was once a news anchor at this very station, WNN, continues to claim innocence even while preaching blasphemy and lies against our leader and messiah, Franco Macalousso, and the One Nation Earth government he has instituted for the good of all mankind."

Behind her the crowd set up another loud and sustained scream.

"This is Stacy Gruber," the reporter shouted into her mike, "coming to you live from the Court of Justice!"

J. T., his fingernails black with grime, reached over and switched off the set, looking around at the others. His wife met his gaze, her eyes welling up with tears. "I can't believe it," she said softly. "Helen . . . she's still alive."

Tony Goss shook his head. "I bet she wishes she wasn't," he said between pursed lips. "They're going to destroy her in court . . . and then kill her to satisfy those animals on the street."

"Score another point for Macalousso's regime," his brother interjected with bitter irony.

"I can't imagine what she must be going through," Selma reflected, "having to face a world that believes she's a cold-blooded killer." Her voice dropped to a hoarse whisper. "God, help her."

"God helps those who help themselves," J. T. retorted angrily. "They call us terrorists. Well, maybe it's time we lived up to our reputation."

"J. T., honey," Sherri said, her voice tinged with worry. "What are you saying?"

J. T. turned to look at his wife. How many times he wished he could give her the simple things that made a woman feel safe and secure: a home, money in the bank, children. Instead, they lived like hunted creatures of the night, crouching in the darkness, running from the shadows. The thought only made him more angry. "I'm saying we can't just sit here while they crucify Helen," he spat. "We should be trying to help her escape. Sure, she'll be heavily guarded, but with a solid plan—"

"That's crazy," Sherri interrupted. "We've lost enough good men and women, J. T. We've got to conserve our strength. Wait for God to give us direction."

J. T. pulled away from her grasp. "That's your best option?" he demanded. "I've got news for you, Sherri." He turned to the others. "I've got news for all of you. Our little message of hope isn't going to keep our sister alive. The time has come to take real action, to show Macalousso and his goons that we're willing and able to fight back!"

Tony stood, stirred by J. T.'s words. "Imagine what a blow it would be to Macalousso, after all the publicity around this trial, if we were to snatch his star defendant right out from under his nose."

"Violence is the only language these people understand," J. T. added urgently. "Black eye for black eye. Broken tooth for broken tooth."

Selma stood now, her eyes flashing with emotion. "Nobody wants to strike back at our enemies worse than I do," she insisted. "They murdered my husband, my precious Frank, right in front of my eyes." She shuddered at the memory, then straightened up, steeling herself. "But that would be sending exactly the wrong message. There has to be another way."

J. T. shook his head vehemently. "If there is," he muttered, "I for one am tired of waiting to find out what God might have in mind."

∽

Sitting in a sterile and windowless holding cell far removed from the tumult of the street outside, Helen Hannah was lost in thoughts and questions of her own. If she had somehow been able to hear what her friends and fellow freedom fighters were so urgently discussing, it would have been no easier for her to reach the right conclusion. Should they risk all to save her from the fate Franco Macalousso had decreed? Should they take up violence to meet the violence that had driven them underground, far away from the comfort and security of their former lives? They were dilemmas and choices that brought with them new sets of problems and challenges. And for right now, Helen Hannah had enough of both to keep her busy.

The echoing sounds of a heavy steel door being slowly

opened outside her cell stirred Helen from her lonely contemplation. Footsteps approached and across the room, the
guard who sat in a chair reading a newspaper quickly stood
up and snapped to an attentive stance. A key was heard fit-
ting into the lock and, after a moment, two figures were
revealed standing in the doorway. One, by his uniform,
Helen guessed was a Justice Department guard. The other,
in an expensive suit with a tasteful silk tie and an alligator-
skin briefcase, was just as certainly a lawyer. Helen assumed
she was about to meet her defense attorney.

"Leave us alone," Mitch ordered both guards.

"But we have orders," protested the one standing next to
him. "She's a very dangerous—"

"We have the right to private consultation," Mitch
snapped back. "Or do I have to get Ms. Thorne on the
phone?"

At the sound of that name, the guard swallowed hard.

"Look," Mitch continued in a softer tone, reaching into
his pocket and tossing over a set of car keys. "If anything
happens you can keep my Mercedes. It's the pearl-gray 760
in the lot." The guard caught the keys and signaled to his
partner. Both exited as Mitch sat down at a small table in
one corner of the room, nodding for Helen to join him.
"You must be Helen Hannah," he said with smile that suggested utter sincerity.

"How'd you guess?" replied Helen sarcastically, then
glanced at the manacles around her hands and feet. "Was it
my jewelry?"

Mitch stuck out his hand. "Mitchell Kendrick," he said. "I've been . . . retained to represent you."

Helen looked down at the hand, on the back of which had been tattooed a small 666. Mitch, noticing where her eyes fell, withdrew his hand quickly, sliding his cuff down over the mark, and cleared his throat. Opening his brief-case, he took out a sheaf of paper. "According to this filing," he explained, "you've been charged with the highest crime of One Nation Earth—hatred of humanity."

Helen stared at him impassively, as if inviting him to make his own judgment about her guilt or innocence.

Mitch met her gaze for a moment, then dropped his eyes. "Look," he muttered, "everyone knows you are one of the ringleaders of the Haters. According to the law that means you deserve to die. But Mr. Macalousso is prepared to be merciful. If you take the mark like all the rest of us, you can walk out of here a free woman. Today. No ques-tions asked. If not—"

"If not," Helen echoed, "then my blood is on my own hands. Is that what you're saying, Mr. Kendrick?"

Mitch sighed. "Look," he answered after a moment. "I don't care what you do. You got yourself into this mess and I don't think the best attorney in the world could get you out." He paused. "Not the way they've got this trial set up, anyway. So my best professional advice to you, Miss Hannah, is to take the mark and forget the whole thing. It's not as bad as you think. Believe me."

Seconds ticked by as Helen continued to fix the lawyer

with a stony stare. Then, her eyes slowly closed and her head bowed.

Mitch let out an exasperated snort. "If you're praying to your God for an answer or deliverance or something, don't bother. I can assure you, even if He existed, He's going to leave you to twist in the wind on this one."

"You have no idea what He is capable of," Helen replied with tight-lipped determination. "He is watching right now, listening to everything we say. He knows what will happen to me. And to you."

Mitch laughed derisively, but he couldn't help glancing nervously up at the ceiling of the cell. "If what you say is true," he said, standing up and closing his briefcase, "then He'd probably be the first one to tell you that without taking the mark, you haven't got a prayer, Ms. Hannah."

"That's where you're wrong, Mr. Kendrick," Helen shot back. "I've always got a prayer." She watched as the lawyer pounded on the door and was let out into the narrow corridor beyond. As his footsteps faded away, Helen heard her own words echoing in her ears. "How is it, Lord," she whispered, "that I can sound so brave when I feel so frightened?"

Chapter 4

A TOWERING STEEL PLAQUE bearing the One Nation Earth crest hung above the packed courtroom, setting the tone of absolute authority and implacable justice for the proceedings about to get under way. But as solemn and intimidating as the symbol of Franco Macalousso's power might have been, it could not diminish the excited babble of the onlookers, who were squeezed like sardines into the visitors' galleries on either side of the hall. The aura of anticipation was enhanced by the brilliant lights of TV cameras glaring down on the judge's bench as well as on the prosecution and defense tables. The solemn ONE guards stationed at every entrance and exit of the courtroom added to the sense that something earthshaking was about to commence under the avid gaze of a waiting world. For this moment, this room was the exact center of the globe, and those who filled its seats and milled around in its aisles were well aware of their presence in the epicenter of history.

The hubbub subsided quickly as the huge oak doors

swung wide to admit Mitch Kendrick and Victoria Thorne, walking side by side to their respective places in front of the judge's bench. Mitch, all business, sat down immediately and began poring over his notes while a considerably more relaxed Victoria gave an off-the-cuff interview to the anxiously waiting news crew. After a moment, she noticed her adversary hard at work and, breaking away, approached Mitch stealthily from behind. Tapping him on the shoulder, she watched with wicked glee as, startled, the distracted lawyer jumped with a yelp, scattering his papers across the desk. He turned, glaring at her.

"Just want to remind you to look surprised when I mop the floor with you," Victoria said with a smirk.

Behind them a buzzer sounded loudly and every head in the courtroom craned to watch as a shackled Helen Hannah was led through what looked like a specially modified metal detector and, flanked by two beefy and heavily armed guards, walked slowly toward the defense table. Softly, almost imperceptibly, the silence was broken by the sound of murmurs and hissing. It rose quickly to become a hateful clamor with murderous shouts from the well-dressed crowd, and increased further still until the onlookers were howling for Helen's blood like a pack of rabid dogs.

Under the unblinking eye of the television cameras, Helen did her best to hide her terror but her trembling hands, pale skin, and wide eyes gave her away. For the first time she was grateful for the guards that surrounded her. Without them, she would surely have been torn limb from limb by this rabid mob. As she headed toward her seat, she caught a glimpse of a hulking man fixing her with a look of pure hate and clutching something tightly to his chest beneath his jacket.

Mitch and Victoria watched the procession and as Helen approached, the defense attorney gave his opponent a cynical look. "Was setting up the mark detector your idea?" he asked, referring to the omnipresent machine that scanned the 666 symbol emblazoned on the hand of every citizen who had pledged allegiance to One Nation Earth.

Victoria shrugged. "You know it's required by law in all public places," she parried. "I can't help it if it makes your client look as guilty as sin."

"Of course not," Mitch replied. "Especially with all the television cameras recording the whole thing."

"This is a performance, Mitch," Victoria reminded him in a fierce whisper, "and this courtroom is a theater. Try and remember that."

She moved across the aisle to her desk as Helen took a seat next to Mitch without looking at him or anyone else. Her eyes fixed on the tabletop, her demeanor made Mitch wonder if she was praying again. He admitted with a sigh that whatever it was she believed, she had real faith in it.

The bailiff entered though a side door and cleared his throat. "Hear ye, hear ye," he intoned. "The One Nation Earth Supreme Court of Justice is now in session, the Honorable Judge Thorton Wells presiding."

The courtroom members dutifully rose to their feet as

Wells, looking stern and regal in his heavy black robes, entered and took his position on the raised platform of his bench. In quick succession two other associate judges emerged and took their places on either side of him.

"Case number 657-908," the bailiff continued, "the People of One Nation Earth versus Helen Hannah on the charge of crimes against humanity."

More murmuring was heard from the gallery until the judge shot the crowd a warning look and the grumbling subsided.

"Will the accused please rise?" the bailiff said, turning to the defense table.

Helen and Mitch got to their feet.

"How do you plead?" Judge Wells asked, his voice reverberating through the high ceilings of the courtroom.

Mitch stepped forward. "We, uh, plead 'Not guilty,' Your Honor," he said in a barely audible voice.

Again muttering rose from the onlookers, loud this time and threatening to break out into another demonstration of loathing for the defendant.

Judge Wells pounded his gavel and the sound was deafening. "Order!" he boomed. "I'll have no disturbances while my court is in session," he warned.

The chastened crowd quickly stilled.

Wells turned to Victoria. "Ms. Prosecutor," he ordered, "please proceed."

"Of course, Your Honor," she replied, taking her place in front of her table. She stood silent for a long moment, letting the dramatic tension build. When at last she spoke, every eye and all ears, both inside the room and beyond its walls to the far horizons, were riveted on the beautiful and brilliant lawyer.

"Your Honor," she began in ringing tones, then turned and looked deliberately into the lens of the nearest camera. "Citizens of the world, we are here today to judge the guilt or innocence of this woman." She pointed to Helen Hannah, her arm as straight and direct as an arrow. "But it is not just Helen Hannah who is on trial here today. It is each and every one of her kind, all those who, like her, profess to believe in a vengeful and irrational God and the so-called Son He sent to supposedly die for all the sins of mankind. But Helen Hannah and those like her are not just on trial for giving over their hearts and minds to an ancient and dangerous superstition. *No.*" Her voice rose sharply at the word. "She and the rest of the Haters are here today charged with poisoning the human race with their lies and deceit. One Nation Earth intends to prove over the course of this trial, beyond the shadow of any reasonable doubt, that Helen Hannah and her ilk do indeed hate you and hate me and hate all of us."

She pointed directly at the camera's unblinking eye even as the cameraman moved in for the tightest possible close-up. Another long silence followed and when she broke it, Victoria had assumed a tone of sweet reason, as if she were talking directly to a beloved child.

"I want you to imagine something with me," she invited.

"I want you to imagine, just for a moment, that we're all together on one boat in the middle of a vast, uncharted ocean. That boat, ladies and gentlemen, is this fragile planet we call Earth. And the vast water around us is the ocean of time. Now imagine that suddenly, up ahead of us, is a huge whirlpool . . . "

In homes and offices, bars and restaurants, hotels and schoolrooms across seven continents, the populace of the planet pictured together the enormous sucking cylinder of water that Victoria evoked.

"If we don't do something very soon," she continued, her voice dropping to a low and ominous tone, "we're all going to perish in the whirlpool." Again she paused for maximum effect and it seemed as if the whole globe held its breath in unison.

"But then," she continued at last, "just at the moment of utmost danger, when all looks most hopeless, something miraculous happens. A leader stands up in our boat and, in the midst of all the panic and despair, this remarkable man, unlike any other who has ever emerged from the human race, begins to speak to us all with wisdom and compassion. His wise words help us to understand that, if we all work together, we can save ourselves and our precarious boat. But only," and she raised her forefinger high as she made her next pronouncement, "if we all, each one of us, do our part. In other words, ladies and gentlemen, this wise leader is telling us that we have a choice. We must unite and live. Or keep to our old ways . . . and die."

Her words were ringing now, rising up to the vaulted ceiling of the courtroom. "Our leader has taught us that, if we all pick up our oars and row together, we can pull away from the mouth of the horrible whirlpool. If we forget our differences and remember that we're all brothers and sisters, we can save ourselves and our planet. But each and every one of us must do his or her part. Because if you're not rowing away from the whirlpool, that can only mean that you're rowing toward it. And that means you are actively working for the destruction of the human race." She stared at Helen Hannah, her eyes flashing fire.

The defendant returned her gaze bravely and for her defiance earned even more hatred from the seething crowd. Once again Helen noticed the hulking man in the overcoat, sitting in the back of the gallery, his eyes seemingly burning two holes into her soul.

With a deliberately measured pace, Victoria returned to her table and picked up a simple wooden oar, brandishing it around the room and directly into the cameras. "Because most of us have followed our leader and picked up our oars," she continued, "we have seen his words come to pass. We have begun to overcome the powerful currents that were dragging us down. Because we were united behind our messiah, we were able to accomplish great things together.

"Yet there are some in the boat who do not row with us. There are some who tell us that the wisdom and courage of our leader is nothing less than a great evil that we must reject. They tell us that what we are doing is wrong, but they don't just use hateful words to make their point. They grab the oars from our hands and try to push us overboard."

To demonstrate her point, the prosecutor dropped the oar onto the marble floor where it clattered noisily, echoing through the silent chamber. Even before the sound subsided, Victoria was once again pointing accusingly at Helen Hannah and saying, "This woman is one of those people! This woman once came to you over the television and claimed to be telling you the truth. But the truth is, my fellow citizens, that Helen Hannah is interested in only one thing and that is plunging our fragile boat deep into that deadly whirlpool!"

Helen never flinched even as Victoria's words resounded around the room, setting off a fresh round of shouts and cries.

At Helen's side, however, Mitch looked grim and pale. It was only now that he was beginning to realize the peril of the part into which he had been cast. Would the hatred the whole world felt for his client spread to her lawyer as well? Suddenly Mitch wanted more than anything else to slink out of the courtroom and back to his office, to pick up his life where it had been so rudely interrupted.

"Helen Hannah doesn't care about you or me or anything other than her imaginary God!" Victoria shouted above the clamor of the crowd. "If we want to survive, if we want our boat to reach safe harbor, then we must find her and her kind guilty as charged—guilty of the brutal slaying of innocent children by terrorist acts against One Nation Earth!"

Reaching over, she picked up another prop from her desk. It was a badly damaged child's teddy bear, its stuffing sticking out from its torn fur, singed and battered. Victoria was silent for a long and suspenseful moment as she stared at the toy and the cameras moved in to catch the glistening of tears in her eyes. When she looked up again, it was directly at the vast television audience. "On that charge of crimes against humanity, there is only one verdict that does justice to what this woman and her kind have done: guilty! All Christians must pay the price for their deeds. And for the common good of us all, the sentence must be the most severe we can apply: death!"

The crowd, frenzied now, picked up the last word and began chanting it, louder and louder. Rising from the seats in the gallery, the mob began moving toward the defense table as guards tried to restrain it.

Judge Wells pounded futilely with his gavel. "Order!" he shouted over the tumult. "Order in the court!"

Helen too was standing now, a fire of fury burning in her eyes. "This trial is a mockery!" she declared, her defiant voice lifting above the others. "There's no justice here!"

Mitch grabbed her arm and pulled her back into her seat. "Shut up!" he hissed. "You're just making it worse."

"It can't be any worse!" Helen whispered back, "because you're one of them too. You're supposed to be on my side, but you're just pretending. Aren't you?"

Mitch swallowed hard, trying desperately to answer her question and still maintain some shred of his integrity. It was at that moment that complete pandemonium erupted in the courtroom as, with a savage cry, the hulking man leaped down from the gallery, brandishing the scissors he had concealed beneath his coat. "You killed my daughter!" he screamed, making a lunge for Helen. "You killed my little girl!"

Mitch jumped in front of his client to protect her and in the next second, a phalanx of guards had swarmed over the assailant and wrestled him to the ground where he continued to shout out his accusation between choked sobs.

From the bench, the judge's gavel sounded like rifle shots and Mitch turned to stare into the horror-stricken face of Helen Hannah. *She is right,* he thought to himself. *This isn't a trial. This is a legal lynching.*

Chapter 5

HELEN SAT TREMBLING in the stark confines of the holding cell while outside the echoes of the clamoring crowd could still be heard. Exhausted by the morning's events, she rested her head in her hands, trying to find the strength to pray, although how God would deliver her from this present peril was a challenge that shook her to the core of her faith. If she ever had any doubt about the hopelessness of her situation, the spectacle in the courtroom that she had just endured dispelled it forever. She was in mortal danger and nothing less than a miracle would deliver her now. Miracles, it seemed, were in short supply in the brave new world of Franco Macalousso.

Even as she began to summon the strength to ask God to sustain her for the next installment of her ordeal, the cell door opened and her lawyer entered, an exasperated look on his face. He sat down in the chair across the table from her and for a long moment simply stared at her, as if his eyes could express more than his words could ever say.

"I'm sorry," said Helen at last. "But you must know as well as I do that this trial is a sham."

"I don't know any such thing," Mitch insisted, although as he broke his gaze, his face flickered with a shadow of guilt. "All I know is that I'm never going to be able to run this trial if you keep behaving like this. It's almost as if you want them to convict you."

"I notice you said 'run the trial,'" Helen observed softly. "Whatever happened to *winning* the trial?"

"That's entirely up to you," Mitch countered. "Your fate is completely in your own hands."

"My fate is in God's hands," Helen replied, surprising even herself with the confidence of her words.

"Well, in that case, you sure don't need me," Mitch responded sardonically. "You and God can lose this case all on your own." He leaned forward, an intense look on his face. "Listen to me, Helen," he continued. "I know what I'm talking about. God is not going to save you. You're on your own. Please, for your sake, for all of our sakes, take the mark. It's not so bad. You'll be free. You can start a new life."

Helen just stared back at him as if he were the one to be pitied.

"Okay!" Mitch exclaimed with a snarl. "There's nothing I can say to shake this crazy belief that you have. I know that. I've been around your kind."

He stood up and began pacing the small perimeter of the room. "But this isn't about words in some book, about an afterlife in the sweet by-and-by. This is about real life. Your life."

"You mean my life now, on this earth?" Helen asked, although she already knew the answer." She snapped her fingers. "That's gone, Mr. Kendrick. It's over in an instant. What matters is the life waiting for us all on the other side. Eternal life, life with God."

Mitch snorted with derision. "You want eternal life?" he spat. "You're so anxious to leave this life for a better one? Fine. But do me a favor. Don't preach to me. I know all about the suicide cult of you Christians and it makes me sick! I'm sorry that I ever got sucked into this mess, but I'll tell you one thing. Whatever Mitch Kendrick begins, Mitch Kendrick finishes. And that's more than I can say for your so-called Almighty God. Any God who demands the kind of loyalty that sends people happily to their deaths is a menace to society. Maybe it's time someone made the case for good, old-fashioned human responsibility."

Keys jangled at the door and a guard poked his head in. "Court's back in session," he announced.

Helen rose, the chains that bound her rattling as she walked. At the door she turned again to face her lawyer. "Well, Mr. Kendrick," she said with resignation in her voice, "now is your chance to prove that humans can be responsible."

∾

The courtroom had been restored to a semblance of order by the time Helen and Mitch entered and made their way slowly to the defense table, but the looks of seething hatred and barely restrained violence that followed them down the aisle were menacing as the shouts and screams the angry mob had unleashed at the last session. Judge Wells cast a stern look around the room as a warning against any more unseemly outbreaks and Mitch could not help but admire how he was playing the part of the unbiased justice to perfection. But now it was time for Mitch to play his part and the feeling of anxiety that grumbled in the pit of his stomach was an unfamiliar one. He was used to doing whatever it took to win a case and get ahead. Why was he having such a hard time submitting to the scripted outcome of this trial, the most important of his career?

Before Mitch had time to consider the answer to that question, the judge pounded his gavel, signaling that court was back in session. "Defense," he intoned, turning to Mitch, "you may proceed with your opening statement."

Mitch cleared his throat and stepped out from behind the table, making his way to the front of the judge's high bench. "Your Honor," he began in a clear, ringing tone and then turned to the audience. "Ladies and gentlemen, people of One Nation Earth." He paused, milking the dramatic effect as effectively as Victoria had. "Let me begin by acknowledging right here and now that my esteemed colleague for the prosecution is absolutely right in what she has to say about this trial and my client."

The cameras turned immediately to Victoria, who made no effort to hide the smug smile on her face. No one in the worldwide media noticed Judge Wells looking down surreptitiously at the script in front of him to make sure that the young attorney was following his lines.

"We live in a wonderful and exciting new world today," Mitch continued. "We are all citizens of one planet, passengers in one boat, to use Ms. Thorne's apt analogy. We must all row together if we are to reach our destination." He turned back to face Helen. "And that is exactly the problem. Not all of us are rowing. Not all of us are doing our part. There are some, such as my client here, who refuse to do their part, refuse to put aside their antiquated beliefs in a vengeful and unreasonable God and work with the rest of us for the common good."

It was Helen's turn now to face the cameras, as the blood drained from her features and a look of white-hot fury came over her pale face.

"Instead," Mitch continued, ignoring his client's obvious anger, "they continue in their selfish ways. They will not give up their superstitions or their attempts to seduce others into believing what they believe."

Helen, her lips drawn in a thin line, started to rise, but Mitch, seeing her furious movement, raised his voice as he continued to press his point. He wasn't about to let the defendant speak for herself. He had his own strategy for the next crucial phase of her trial. "But I would submit you, ladies and gentlemen and people of One Nation Earth, that although such unfortunates as Helen Hannah can cause great destruction and impede the progress we have all made together, they are ultimately not to blame for their irrational and antisocial actions."

Victoria Thorne and Judge Wells exchanged a quick and worried look. Whatever Mitch Kendrick had up his sleeve, it most definitely was not part of the well-laid plan that had been worked out to the last detail. The judge shot Mitch a warning glance, but there was nothing to do now in front of the eyes of the world but to give the lawyer free rein. It was a problem that would have to be dealt with later, and most severely.

"Helen Hannah can't be held responsible for her actions, any more than a trained animal can be held responsible for doing the tricks its master commands," Mitch continued.

The audience members shifted in their chairs, curious now about the direction the trial had suddenly taken.

"Helen Hannah, and the others like her, are only following orders—the orders she imagines she hears from her almighty taskmaster. She is only a pawn in a deadly game." Mitch turned back to the judge, raising his arms in a grand gesture. "I submit to Your Honor that, instead of prosecuting this mere pawn, this mindless puppet, we should be holding accountable her Lord and Master. He is the true criminal, the real force that is holding back the progress and enlightenment of One Nation Earth!"

"I fail to see what this has to do with the crimes your client is accused of committing," sputtered Judge Wells, his eyes sparking a dire warning to Mitch. "What is your point exactly, Counselor?"

"My point is this, Your Honor," Mitch shot back as the courtroom listened in utter silence. "We have the wrong criminal in the courtroom here today."

A murmur ran through the gallery at his words. Helen, from her place at the defense table, sank back into her seat, the anger in her face now replaced by fear and confusion.

"This trial shouldn't be about the terrorist acts she may or may not have committed," Mitch asserted. "This trial should follow the chain of command to the highest levels, bringing to justice the one who has deceived Helen Hannah and all the other Haters into believing they are saving mankind and not destroying it!"

Every camera now shared the same tight shot of Mitch. From across the room Victoria caught his attention and drew a finger across her neck. *Pull the plug,* her gesture signaled, *or we'll pull it for you.*

Mitch ignored her. "Helen Hannah and those like her," he continued, "are the deluded followers of a Christian God who for centuries has held men and women in bondage." Mitch stared straight into the cameras. "This so-called God is the one who encourages her and her coconspirators to create havoc in our society. Make no mistake about it: Helen Hannah is no more responsible for her actions than a robot who has been programmed to destroy. It's her Lord and Master who must be called into account." His voice was raised to a shout as he declared, "Let's put God on trial!"

Around him the gallery erupted in cheers, applause,

and stomping feet. The judge and prosecutor were already standing, Victoria shouting objections and Wells pounding his gavel. "Counsel," the judge commanded, shouting to be heard above the tumult, "in my chambers! Now!"

cło

Victoria stood by the spacious window of the judge's book-lined window, her arms crossed and her foot tapping, while Wells fumed and paced, awaiting the arrival of the disobedient defense lawyer. Escorted by the judge's secretary, Mitch felt like a schoolboy called on the carpet for playing hooky except for one overwhelming difference—the stakes he was playing with involved people's lives, including his own.

"Just what do you think you're doing out there, young man?" Judge Wells demanded as soon as Mitch entered. He picked up the script from his desk and shook it. "Your lines are right here, in black and white. Nothing could be clearer. And that little display you put on out there is just going to make all our jobs that much harder."

"I stand by what I said," Mitch insisted. "We've got to go after the real criminal in this case."

From the deep shadows in a corner of the room a voice could be heard, familiar, yet thoroughly intimidating. It was the voice of authority, pure and absolute. It was the voice of Franco Macalousso. When he had entered or how he had arrived was a complete mystery to the other three in the room. But now was not the time for questions. Now was the time to hear and obey.

"And who," Macalousso asked in a cool, calm tone of voice, "might that criminal be, Mitch?"

Judge Wells seemed to shrink inside his black robes, quaking with fear and awe and the messiah stepped from the shadows and made his way across the room. "Your Eminence," the judge began, his voice quaking.

Macalousso raised a hand, instantly silencing him. "Please," the world leader said, an indulgent smile playing across his thin lips, "indulge me, Mr. Kendrick. Why did you choose not to follow the . . . instructions that were laid out for you today?"

"Because," Mitch replied stubbornly, although his voice trembled, "I think we're going after the wrong offender."

"Listen, Mitch," Victoria said, stepping forward angrily. "What makes you think any of us cares what you think? This isn't your show!"

Macalousso silenced her with a single sharp glance. "I can handle this from here, Ms. Thorne," he said, a slight note of warning in his voice. He turned back to Mitch. "Please," he said graciously, "continue."

"Thank you, Your Eminence," Mitch replied, shooting a satisfied glance in Victoria's direction. "The way I look at it, if we prosecute Helen Hannah—" he pointed to the papers in Judge's Wells's hand, "according to that scenario, all we've done is make the problem worse."

"How so?" asked Macalousso, his eyes fixed intently on Mitch.

"Let's say she's convicted and executed, according to plan," Mitch continued. "She's going to be more powerful dead than alive. All we'll have done is create a martyr for the Haters to rally around. A freedom fighter willing to die for what she believes in is a powerful symbol. Before it's all over, the legend we create about Helen Hannah may even draw more people to her cause. We've got to take this trial to the next stage. We've got to hold her God responsible for the actions of His followers. The followers are doing only what they think their Master wants them to do."

Victoria and Judge Wells carefully watched Macalousso from the corner of their eyes, trying to gauge his response. Whatever he might be thinking would quickly become what they would think.

Macalousso nodded, but his face was impassive.

Mitch swallowed hard and pressed on. "Think of all you've done in so short a time, sir," he suggested. "Think of how you've taken this planet from the verge of utter chaos and destruction into a bright new day of peace and prosperity. Since you arrived two years ago, you've accomplished more than the God of Helen Hannah has in countless eons. Unless we handle this trial right, there's a real danger all that progress could be lost. We can't let them win, sir. We've got to show them who the real savior of mankind is."

A long moment passed, with the only sounds the passing of traffic far below and the muffled ticking of a clock on the judge's desk. Macalousso, deep in thought, seemed to be ignoring the presence of the others in the room until at last he looked up and gave Mitch an approving nod. "Your zeal becomes you, young man," he said. "It's true. The world's citizens serve me not because of their hate for Helen Hannah and her kind. They serve me because I have given them their hearts' desires. The time has come to show them who really has their best interests at heart . . . and who will deliver on the promises he has made."

Turning to Judge Wells and Victoria, the sinister messiah continued, "This trial must become a judgment of God Himself. It is only then that Hannah and the rest of Haters will be seen as guilty by association." His eyes were alight now, from what source the others could not guess. "This will be a victory I will cherish for all eternity!" He laughed, a sound that sent a sudden cold chill down Mitch's spine. "God will be found guilty of crimes against His own creation and His judges will be that very creation."

He nodded to Victoria. "Prepare a press conference immediately to inform the media of the change. We're accusing God Himself, through the actions of His followers." He took the script from the Wells's hand and tossed it in a nearby wastebasket. "Let's give Mr.Kendrick a little room to improvise, shall we?" he said with a grin.

Mitch in turn smiled, an expression in marked contrast to the scowl on Victoria's face. Suddenly, this was personal.

Chapter 6

THE GRIM AND NEON-LIGHTED HOLDING CELL was beginning to seem like the closest thing to a sanctuary Helen could find in her life. It was the only place she could be alone, the only place she could gather her strength and seek the comfort of the Lord through prayer. She found that she actually looked forward to the heavy door slamming behind her. This was where she could find solace and the courage to face her ordeal, looking for provision from one moment to the next through her communion with the Author and Finisher of her faith.

But after the events of that afternoon, Helen found it hard to focus her attention on God. The trial had taken a perilous new turn, and it did so not through any devices of her enemies, but through the strategy of her supposed defender. As long as the prosecution had been directed toward her, Helen felt she could endure anything. But to slander and defame the name of God—that was arrogance beyond anything she could imagine.

It was at that moment that Mitch entered, and from

the bounce in his step and the bright expression on his face she could tell that he was more than a little pleased with himself.

"What do you think you're doing out there?" she demanded, jumping to her feet. "This trial is supposed to be about me! I suggest you leave God out of it. For your own good."

"Is that a threat?" Mitch asked. "Because if it is, save your breath."

Helen shook her head in disbelief. "Do you really hate God that much?' she asked incredulously.

"I hate what He makes people do in His name," Mitch promptly replied.

"And what's that?" Helen challenged him. "To love your neighbor? To stand up for the truth? To put others before yourself?"

"I was thinking more about dying for a useless cause," Mitch said bitterly. "If your idea of loving your neighbor and putting others first includes killing innocent children, then you're even more deluded then I thought you were."

"I never killed anyone," came Helen's even reply. "No bombs. No bullets. I've been set up. We all have. And you know it."

"Oh, do I?" Mitch answered, rolling his eyes with exaggerated impatience. "Let me tell you something, lady. I know one thing. Your God has a lot to answer for. And I intend to be the one asking the questions."

Helen shook her head sadly. "You still don't get it, do

you?" she said, with genuine empathy. "This trial was never about me. And it's never going to be about God."

Mitch snorted. "Then why don't you tell me exactly what it is about?"

"It's about Franco Macalousso," Helen said. "It's about Lucifer himself, making war on God. It's about the battles that are going on, every minute of every day, in the hearts and souls and minds of every human being on this planet. Macalousso wants to assure that anyone and everyone who won't submit to the mark of 666 is a terrorist bent on destroying the world. He is trying to make it seem as if the only way for the human race to survive is to wipe out anyone who disagrees with him. Does that sound like a savior to you?"

"So let me get this straight," Mitch responded. "You're saying that Franco Macalousso, the most powerful man in the world, the most beloved leader in human history, is personally trying to set you up. The one person who has given countless people hope for the future has taken the trouble to frame little old Helen Hannah?"

Helen's look was the only answer Mitch needed. "That's quite a claim," he continued. "Would it be too much to ask for a little proof?"

"I have all the proof you'll ever need," Helen replied, her voice brimming with conviction. "The true identity of Franco Macalousso, his one-world government—" Helen grabbed Mitch's hand and pointed to the tattooed numbers etched into his flesh— "even this mark. It's all been foretold in the Bible."

Mitch snatched back his hand. "Give me a break!" he spat. "That book's been banned and you know it. Beside, even if you wanted me to try and prove your case, I'd need a whole lot more than a bunch of fairy tales and bedtime stories. I'd need hard evidence."

A long moment passed before Helen wordlessly took a piece of paper and a pen from the desk and scribbled something down. Thrusting it into Mitch's hands, she sat down and once again buried her head in her hands. Mitch could hear her whispered prayer as he glanced down at the paper he held. An e-mail address was written on it.

༄

Victoria walked along the marble-lined hallways of the One Nation Earth Supreme Court building, the sounds of her high heels echoing high above her in the vaulted ceilings. She turned first one corner, then another, strolling deeper and deeper into the maze of offices and courtrooms until coming at last to a small corridor that emptied out into a dead end. There, a man dressed in dark clothes and wearing heavy wraparound sunglasses that completely obscured his eyes, stood as if waiting for her.

Looking around to make sure they were alone, Victoria spoke in low tones. "We have a problem," she confided to the strange and sinister stranger. "Mitchell Kendrick is his name. He's overstepping his bounds."

The stranger nodded wordlessly, exuding a aura of menace simply standing and listening to his orders.

"I want to persuade Mr. Kendrick that going his own way can prove very hazardous to his health," Victoria continued. "I've been told you are an excellent . . . persuader." She smirked as another nod greeted her words. "But you're not much of a conversationalist, are you?" She turned and began walking down the hall, stopping to throw a parting shot over her shoulder. "You'll rein him in . . . understand?"

But the stranger had already disappeared, leaving the prosecutor to wonder how he had managed to get by her in the narrow, doorless hallway.

◌

Deep below the surface of the teeming city, safe from the prying eyes of ONE security forces, the small, hungry band of resisters sat huddled around the flickering, static-shot picture on their pirated television monitor. The same WNN anchor stood outside the courthouse, talking earnestly into the camera, holding a microphone in one hand.

"Billed as the most important trial of our time," she reported, "the case against Helen Hannah took a startlingly new and epic turn today in what must be an unprecedented development in legal history. Defense attorney Mitch Kendrick, son of notorious Hater Seth Kendrick, whose execution was widely seen as an devastating setback for the Hater cause, has convincingly argued that his client should not be on trial at all. The real criminal, Kendrick maintains, is the deity Hannah and others mindlessly follow . . . God Himself."

Selma stifled a cry and dismay and jumped up from her seat. "What does that fool lawyer think he's doing?" she demanded.

J. T. slammed his fist into the moth-eaten armchair they had dragged off the street and into their hideout. "They talk about locusts being a plague," he commented bitterly, "the real plague is lawyers." He suddenly stood up in front of the television and addressed the others. "That's it!" he declared. "No more sitting around waiting for fire to fall from the sky. It's time we put our faith into action!"

"J. T., no," pleaded his wife, Sherri. "Please don't do anything crazy. We've got to wait until we're sure."

"I'm tired of waiting," J. T. countered vehemently. "All my life I've been told to wait. 'Wait for this. Wait for that.' The time for waiting is over. God wants us to act!"

"How can you be so sure?" Sherri asked him, with fear sparkling in her eyes. "Have you even prayed about it?"

"You and Selma don't have a monopoly on God's will," her husband replied with irritation. "Sometimes God calls us to action, to sacrifice, to risk everything for what's right! I don't need prayer to tell me that."

He turned back to the television. "If it's fire and brimstone they want, it's fire and brimstone they're going to get." He stormed down to the far end of the platform, losing himself in the shadows of the deserted station.

The others watched him go, their faces reflecting the struggle his words had sparked in their hearts and minds.

Suddenly, from a computer terminal next to them, a small beeping sound interrupted their somber contemplation.

"E-mail," Jake Goss announced, "incoming." Hitting a few keystrokes, he waited until the message scrolled up onto the screen. With a tone of surprise he read out loud, "Sometimes it may be best to cast your pearls before swine." He turned to the others. "That's the code to send Sweig's tape," he whispered.

"Who sent it?" asked Tony.

Jake glanced back at the screen, as if he could hardly credit what his eyes were telling him. "It's from Helen's lawyer," he said at last.

ൟ

The city nightscape leaked its pale glow through the windows of Mitch's office, where the lawyer sat beneath the light of a computer monitor, clicking keys with his breath held. He was half-convinced that he was crazy for even trying to call up the e-mail address Helen had given him and more than once, he had hesitated as he typed out the letters and symbols. But it was too late to stop now. Whatever he was supposed to learn about the guilt or innocence of Helen Hannah and her band of Haters was about to become crystal clear. Mitch couldn't help but wonder whether the truth would set her, or him, free.

Sending his cursor to the e-mail attachment he clicked his mouse and watched as the screen went blank. A moment later, a powerfully built man with a crew cut and a weather-worn face appeared. In one hand he held a silver badge that established his identity as a One Nation Earth security operative. In the other, he clutched a small black box with a button built into its top.

"My name is Carl Sweig," a tinny voice announced from the computer speakers. "I am former One Nation Earth Agent 077. What I hold in my hand is a standard-issue ONE detonator."

The video camera zoomed in on the agent's face and for the first time, Mitch could see the haunted look in his eyes.

"I used this a devise exactly like this," Sweig continued, "to blow up a bus full of school children four months ago. It was an action that was subsequently blamed on the Haters. They had nothing to do with it. My orders came from the highest levels of the ONE hierarchy."

The camera was in very tight now, and Mitch was surprised to see a glint of tears forming in the corner of the agent's eyes. *Whatever could make a man like this cry*, he thought, *must be a burden too terrible to carry.*

"The purpose of this tape," Sweig continued, "is to prove, beyond any shadow of a doubt, that my superiors at ONE masterminded each and every one of the attacks that were later blamed on the Haters. It was my job to carry out those attacks—" his voice choked for a moment and he paused until he could regain his composure. "It's a job I can't do anymore . . ."

༄

In a cluttered and dimly lit room, a small, overweight man in a dirty lab coat scurried around, making last-minute adjustments on a haphazard collection of medical equipment clustered around a rusty operating table with padded restraints. A man lay prone on the table. Lowering a pair of microsurgical goggles over his bloodshot eyes, Colin McMahon wiped the sweat from his bald head as he talked in a rapid whisper to his patient on the table.

"It's going to feel as if your hands have been pressed in a waffle iron once the freeze wears off," he said. "I've got some painkillers to ease off the hurt. Cost you, though. Nothing's cheap these days."

"I'll manage," said J. T. from his position on the operating table.

"Just a couple more minutes," said the outlaw doctor as he leaned in his work and J. T. winced with pain. Finally, McMahon loosened the restraints and stepped back to admire his handiwork. "One of my better efforts, If I don't say so myself," he remarked as he pulled up a gurney on which sat a computer screen. A few swift keystrokes and the doctor called up an extensive file with the heading "Allegiance Databank." Typing rapidly, he giggled and continued talking to himself.

J. T. did his best to ignore the strange little man. His hand was beginning to throb.

"There," said McMahon at last, finishing his typing

with a flourish. "You're all registered. It's as if you walked into a ONE center and took the mark officially. You won't have any problems with detectors or credit checks. That I can guarantee." Switching off his equipment, he turned to his patient with a greedy look in his eyes.

Pulling out a handful of gold coins, J. T. handed them over and the doctor eagerly began counting them. It was hard to ignore the 666 etched into the back of his own hand.

"Just make sure you don't breathe a word about this to anyone," McMahon cautioned as J. T. stood to leave, his hand throbbing now.

"No offense, Doc," he said as he opened the door, letting in the garish neon lights of the street and the noise and smells of a derelict downtown neighborhood. "But it's not something I'll be bragging about."

"No offense taken," said the doctor, even now preoccupied with counting his gains. A moment passed as McMahon lovingly handled each coin, biting them to test their authenticity, then secreting them away in a hidden pouch deep within his lab coat. Behind him the sound of street noises could be heard again as the door opened on its squeaking hinges.

"Change your mind about those painkillers?" he asked without turning around.

"Not exactly, Doc," came a voice from behind him. "But you may be needing them pretty soon."

McMahon, startled, spun around to find himself staring into the barrel of a gun held by one of three beefy agents, all dressed in ONE field uniforms. Jumping up, the doctor bumped his bald head against the hanging light over the table, sending it swinging and throwing its light in mad angles around the room.

"No! Please, I—"

His pleas were cut short by a deafening eruption of gunfire, the impact of the bullets throwing him back against a rack of operating tools that came crashing down over him as he crumpled to the floor. From out of his hidden pockets, gold coins rolled across the floor as if they were trying to escape his fate.

The agent with the gun stepped forward and, kneeling down, picked up McMahon's limp hand and inspected the 666 symbol. "Cut it off," he ordered his subordinates. "Take it back to the lab." He straightened up. "Search the streets in a ten-block radius," he commanded. "The other one couldn't have gotten too far."

෴

The view from the roof revealed a long vista of ramshackle tenements and condemned buildings. Far beyond, the skyline rose up in the glittering towers of uptown skyscrapers, a world apart from the squalor and poverty of this forgotten district of the metropolis.

Dawn Blushak, the attractive but unkempt woman who had tried without success to win Mitch Kendrick's sympathy, sat huddled on the rooftop around a small fire. Next to her was a lithe, athletic young man, equally smudged and dirty, but with a good-natured and personable air that was evident even amidst the piles of garbage and debris piled on the roof. His name was Dave Sands and he was listening intently as his girlfriend described her frustrating encounter with the legal profession.

"There's nothing else we can do," Dawn sighed. "I tried everything I could think of. He was just too scared of what might happen to help us."

"There's got to be a way," Dave replied, staring deep into the flickering flames and rubbing his hands to keep warm. They both sat in silence for a long moment, lost in thought. "It's crazy," Dave said at last. "I used to have a job, a family. I was a respected member of the community." He held out his arms. "And now look at me." Odor from under his arms made his nose wrinkle. "Man, I sure need a bath," he continued. "And I'm so darned hungry I'd think I pay a hundred bucks for a deep-fried rat right about now."

Dawn shook her head. "Maybe we're making a mistake resisting," she said. "Maybe it's best if we just give in to what they want." She sighed. "I sure hope this big trial clears up a few things. If those Haters really did kill all those kids . . . well, then, I sure don't want to be on their side of the fence."

Dave was staring curiously at the back of his hand. "I wonder," he remarked absently, as if talking to himself. "Maybe if I just got one of those three sixes, they'd let me have a slice of pizza." He closed his eyes dreamily. "I'd sure go for some extra pepperoni . . . "

A sudden noise interrupted their wistful talk, a scraping

of feet on the fire escape behind them. The two scattered quickly, leaving the fire burning and looking for hiding places with well-practiced eyes. Diving into a rusty air vent, Dawn peeked up over the edge of the corroded metal into to see a pair of heavy black boots move by her. A few feet beyond the boots stopped, retraced their steps, and Dawn held her breath as they came to halt directly in front of the duct in which she hid. A moment later, she stifled a gasp as a face dropped down to look at her.

"Don't be afraid," J. T. whispered. "I'm not going to hurt you."

Chapter 7

T HE TURBO-CHARGED SPORTS CAR, a gift that Mitch
had given himself after winning his first big case, roared
up the deserted street and Mitch steered it to the curb in
front of a small building. The engine throbbed as Mitch sat
staring out the window, unsure whether to go through with
this impulsive visit. At last, he shut off the ignition and
opened the door, stepping into the cool night air.

Standing on the sidewalk brought back a flood of memories and Mitch shuddered, as much in reaction to the
images racing through his mind as to the chill of the moon-
less evening. He walked through the rusted fence that bore
a sign that said "Condemned" and walked slowly up to the
door. "Living Word Church," a sign read in the front window. "Pastor Seth Kendrick." Underneath the name was a
simple declaration, powerful and direct, even though its
paint was chipped and peeling: "The Truth Shall Set You
Free."

Mitch stood at the door for a long moment, the rush of
memories now a flood, and he heard again, as if she were

standing right beside him on the porch, the voice of Helen Hannah from earlier that very afternoon: "I've been set up," she had said. "We all have." Her voice had the ring of truth and the look in her eyes was like an open window to her soul. But how could she be telling the truth? How could everything he'd been told about Franco Macalousso and the new world of universal harmony be nothing but a lie?

Mitch couldn't wrap his mind around such a concept and he suddenly felt very tired. He shut his eyes and bowed his head and in that moment, another memory overpowered him. It was so vivid that he almost whimpered as he recalled in exact detail the conversation he had had with his father, in a holding cell almost exactly like the one that now kept Helen Hannah prisoner.

His father had been dressed in prison blues, his hair uncut and his beard thick around his face. But there was the same fierce spark of defiance that had always lighted his eyes whenever he confronted injustice, a spark that only made Mitch more angry with his father's stubborn refusal to do what was reasonable—and save his life in the process.

"Look, Dad," he remembered himself saying impatiently. "I believe you. If you say you're innocent, then that's good enough for me. But there are the people you've been associating with. Those religious fanatics. They don't help your case. I can't help you unless you help yourself and denounce those Christians."

"I can't do that, Son," was his father's even reply. "If I'm innocent, then so are they. And if I'm guilty, then they are too. Guilty of speaking the truth, regardless of the consequences."

"The truth?" Mitch heard himself shouting, the word echoing in his mind. "The truth is you've all been arrested for terrorist activities. They've got evidence, Dad, over-whelming evidence. If you don't separate yourself from this cult you're caught up in, if you don't admit that Jesus is just a figment of someone's twisted imagination . . . " he paused. The consequences were clear enough without him having to spell them out.

Seth Kendrick only shook his head, smiling sadly. "I'm sorry, Son," he said softly. "I'm sorry you have to be caught up in the middle of this. But there's nothing I can do. How can I renounce what I believe, when what I believe gives me a reason to going on living in this world given over to darkness? Don't you see? My faith is all I have. If I deny Jesus, I deny my own existence."

Mitch's eyes had welled with tears. "Please, Dad. Just do what they tell you to do. I couldn't stand it if— " he choked back a sob. "If I lost you."

Seth's eyes too filled with tears as he moved closer and put his arms around his son, a loving embrace that Mitch could feel even now, standing alone in the darkness of his father's abandoned church.

"Seen a ghost?" said a voice behind him and Mitch jumped back, spinning around in fright. It was only then that he recognized the sardonic smile of Victoria Thorne, her face lighted by the wicked gleam in her eyes.

"I would have preferred a ghost," replied Mitch ruefully. "How did you know where to find me?"

Victoria waved away the question. She had her own agenda. "I'm here to pass along a request. A very special request. My superiors at One Nation Earth are asking for your help in locating an important Haters cell."

"And how am I supposed to do that?" replied Mitch, noticing for the first time a man dressed entirely in black leaning against Victoria's car where she had parked next to his on the street.

"Oh, I'm sure you'll find a way," was Victoria's breezy reply. "All you've got to do is gain Helen Hannah's confidence. You're good at getting people to trust you, Mitch. It's one of your more obvious talents. Once she thinks you're on her side, it should be no problem getting her to hand over names, meeting places, license numbers, anything that will help us run these vermin down."

"She'll never betray her friends," Mitch retorted. "I know their people. The one thing you can count on is their loyalty to each other. And to what they believe."

"Don't underestimate yourself, Mitch," purred Victoria. "You've got a way with women. I can attest to that firsthand. Besides," she smirked, "all you have to do is tell her about your poor father and how your heart still bleeds for him. That's sure to get her on your side."

Mitch's eyes narrowed with rage and Victoria, seeing that she had overstepped her bounds, reached out and gently took his hand. Smoothly, imperceptibly, she attached a tiny metallic chip to his wristwatch, even as she stroked the palm of his hand reassuringly. "Mitch," she said in her best approximation of sincerity, "I know you're feeling uncomfortable about all this. The trial would be a tremendous pressure on anyone. But I've got complete confidence in you. And more importantly, so does Franco Macalousso."

"Why doesn't that make me feel better?" asked Mitch sarcastically.

Victoria let go of his hand. "Try to keep an open mind," she advised. "Remember, this case is going to make history. It'll be remembered as a turning point in the evolution of mankind."

"Easy for you to say!" Mitch snapped. "You're on the winning side. You're holding all the cards and you're still cheating."

Victoria took a step back and folded her arms, regarding Mitch as she would a specimen under a microscope. "You know," she said at last, "when you and I were an item I used to admire you—look up to you. I thought you had what it took to get where you wanted to go. That is, until I saw you with your dad. You were too weak to convince him to give up his insane campaign against ONE. Too weak to stop him spouting off about Jesus and forgiveness and all the rest of those lies. You were too weak to save your own father's life, Mitch. That's why you're here tonight, isn't it? To wallow in your self-pity and your weakness?"

"Stop it, Victoria," Mitch said ominously. "Don't say another word."

"You're right, Mitch," Victoria replied with a wicked sneer. "Words aren't enough. Actions always speak louder than words."

As a shocked Mitch looked on helplessly, Victoria gave a quick signal to the silent man standing beside her car. With a few swift, economical movements, the man pulled a gasoline can and a flare gun from the backseat and, walking with grim determination to the side of the church, doused the building in fuel and aimed the flare gun at it.

"No!" shouted Mitch, but it was too late. The gun launched its missile and with a huge intake of oxygen, the old church was a sudden and brilliant inferno. The heat from the fire was so intense that Mitch, shielding his eyes, had to step back toward the street where he turned to watched in sorrow and anger as the last remnant of his former life, and with it the last memories of his father, went up in thick smoke.

"Don't feel bad," Victoria said as she joined him at the curbside. "I did it for you. Mitch. Your attachment to the dangerous criminal who was Seth Kendrick was beginning to become an embarrassment." Her face, by the light of the fire, was a mask of pure and malevolent evil.

∽

From their rooftop hideout, Dawn and Dave watched as in the far distance, a building went up in flames. It was a common occurrence in this part of the city—buildings torched for the meager insurance claim, or by a clumsy crack addict, or simply for the wicked fun of it by any one of the roaming gangs that terrorized the streets. Behind them stood J. T., looking out over the same horizon, lost in memories of his own.

"I was hoping to find someone around here who would remember the old neighborhood," he said at last. "Instead I find you two."

"What did you expect?" Dave retorted. "This place has been a wasteland ever since ONE took over." It was his turn to look around and sigh. "It used to be a nice place to live." He pointed to a boarded-up storefront directly below them. "That used to be my favorite Baskin Robbins. Thirty-one flavors." He licked his lips. "I could sure go for a double scoop of Rocky Road right about now."

J. T. shook his head ruefully. "Well," he said, turning to Dawn, "I guess some things never change."

They shared a laugh as Dave gave them an injured look and the three returned to the small fire they had been tending behind a pile of abandoned furniture on the rooftop. As Dawn stirred the embers and threw in a chair leg, J. T. settled down and turned to his two former neighborhood friends. "Listen, you guys," he said, swallowing hard. "I need help. I am going to break someone out of the One Nation Earth Court and I can't do it alone. There's good pay for anyone who wants to sign up."

"Let me guess," Dawn said, then shot a glance at Dave.

"Yeah, I'm way ahead of you," he chimed in. "You must be trying to spring Helen Hannah." He grinned.

"And we thought you were trying to get something tough accomplished."

"I know it's crazy," responded J. T. with a sheepish grin. "That's why I knew you guys would be perfect for the job. What with Dawn's computer skills and your inside knowledge of ONE, who else would I go to? You're my team, whether you like it or not."

"You might think you have it all worked out," Dawn said, "but you're forgetting one thing. All the money in the world isn't going to do us much good if they won't let us use it."

J. T. nodded. "I know," he said. "But what you could use is a little something that effectively jams the mark detectors."

Dawn and Dave looked at each other. "Now you're talking," Dawn said.

"But we also want food," Dave interjected. "Lots of food!"

J. T. laughed again. "You'll get your food," he promised. "And a place to stay. It won't exactly be Rocky Road, and there's no room service, but hey," he said, looking around, "it's a whole lot better than sleeping out under the smog."

"He's got a point, Dave," Dawn said, turning to her boyfriend. She was surprised to see him already stuffing his dirty clothes into a makeshift backpack.

ତ୍ଵ

Mitch walked wearily into his darkened study and threw his keys and briefcase on the desk. He could still smell the smoke from his father's burning church on his clothes and for the tenth time that night he suppressed his feelings of rage against Victoria. What she had done was nothing more than a vengeful provocation, designed to remind him that she was the one who was in charge, calling the shots and holding his fate dangling between her fingers. It was not a comfortable place to be, not when those well-manicured fingers belonged to a woman as ruthless and ambitious as Victoria Thorne.

He sat down with a sigh at his desk and was about to turn on the light when he sensed the presence of another person in the room. His eyes quickly scanned the shadowy interior even as he stealthily reached into his desk drawer and pulled out a small but deadly revolver.

"Freeze," he said, pointing the gun toward a particularly dark corner of his office. "Freeze, or so help me, you're a dead man."

"A dead man?" a familiar voice echoed. "Oh, I don't think so, Mr. Kendrick." A light near a chair in the corners switched on and Mitch saw the face of Franco Macalousso smiling at him. Between his thumb and forefinger he held a single bullet.

"You'd be needing this to accomplish such a task," Macalousso said smoothly as Mitch stared at him, dumbfounded. "Tell me something," the world leader continued. "Why is it, Mitch, that you keep only one bullet in your gun?" He paused, letting the question sink it. "It's not for simple protection, is it?" He shook his head as Mitch stared dumbly. "No, I didn't think so. Please," he said, pointing to the useless gun in Mitch's hands. "You might as well put that toy away now."

Trembling, Mitch obeyed as Macalousso continued. "I'll bet nobody really knows why, do they, Mitch? Not your clients. Not Miss Thorne. Nobody. You've managed to hide your secrets very well. Those long, dark days at the bottom of a vodka bottle . . . those futile months spent on a shrink's couch . . . all the other hidden sins you'd rather keep buried."

Mitch shuddered at the catalog of his past failures and weaknesses, but Macalousso held up a reassuring hand. "Oh, don't worry," he said smoothly. "No one else knows. You see, I just have a certain . . . sense about these things. It's uncanny really, how accurate I can be."

Without thinking, Mitch reached for a bottle of vodka in his desk drawer and, pouring himself a strong belt of the clear liquid, he drained it off in a single gulp.

"I like you, Mitch," Macalousso continued, twirling the bullet between his fingers. "Self-pity. Self-centeredness. Prideful, ambitious, a vengeful streak, and a powerful hatred of God and everything He stands for. I could use a man with those qualities. It makes for a most delicious combination."

He paused again and Mitch couldn't get over the feeling that he was being sized up, the way a customer in a seafood restaurant sizes up the lobster he'll chose for that evening's dinner.   "You bring to this case a real passion and conviction," Macalousso continued at last. "That's why I know you'll be doing an excellent job for me. Just as you did when your father stood where Helen Hannah stands now." He held up his index finger and wagged it. "But you are also an impetuous young man. You need some boundaries."

Mitch opened his mouth, but no words escaped. "Helen Hannah must never be allowed to testify for God," said Macalousso, his voice quickly turning from benign to menacing. "It is absolutely imperative that she never speak about her faith and convictions in that courtroom. Do I make myself perfectly clear?"

Mitch, his heart pounding in his chest, nodded mutely as Macalousso stood and walked to the desk. Clasping the lawyer's hand in his own, the sinister leader shook it warmly and favored him with a benevolent smile, just as a gracious father gently corrects an errant son.

"Oh, and one more thing, Mitch," he cautioned, still shaking his hand. "I would very much like to have the last word in this trial. Please make a note to call me to the stand as your last witness. I think you'll be very pleased with my testimony."

With a motion as swift as black smoke rising up a chimney, Macalousso turned and disappeared back into the shadows. Mitch, realizing that he had forgotten to breathe during the visit, gasped for air and looked down into the palm of his hand where the single bullet from his gun now lay nestled.

Chapter 8

HELEN WAS SITTING AT HER USUAL PLACE in the holding cell, trying not to think of what this new day in court might have in store for her, when Mitch entered. Before she could open her mouth even to say hello, he gestured for her silence. While she followed his movements with wide eyes, he pulled a small black box from his coat pocket and flipped a switch that set a tiny red light blinking.

"There," he said with a relieved sigh. "We've got some privacy now."

In the basement room far below the holding cell, two ONE agents sitting at a bank of television surveillance monitors were startled to hear a loud squeal coming from one of the observation units. The screen that displayed Helen's cell became suddenly fuzzy and indistinct.

"We got a problem on the Hannah feed," said one the agents. "Better check the cable."

The other, in the midst of eating his breakfast out of a plastic tray, grumbled as he put down his pancakes and got on his knees to crawl beneath the console.

Several floors above them, Mitch smiled reassuringly at Helen as he set the small jamming device on the table between them. "It's a scrambler," he explained to his client. "They've been monitoring all our conversations from day one. But we can talk freely now."

Helen just stared at him, not knowing in that moment whether to believe a single word her lawyer was telling her. Seeing the doubt in her face, he leaned forward and put his hand over hers. "I checked out that e-mail address you gave me," he said with soft intensity. "I watched the tape. I believe you, Helen. I know you didn't kill those kids."

Helen eyes lighted up with joy and welled over with tears, but Mitch was quick to come to the point. "Don't get too hopeful," he cautioned. "There is simply no way I can use something like that in court. I'm telling you now what I told you the first day we met. The only way out of here is with a 666 on your hand."

Helen shook her head adamantly. "There's no way I can do that," she said. "Nothing's going to change that."

"Look, lady!" snapped an exasperated Mitch. "What exactly is it that you want?"

"That's simple," Helen replied evenly. "I want to be faithful to God."

"Right," snorted Mitch derisively. "Just like He's being faithful to you."

Helen shrugged. "Many have suffered more than I have in the service of God," she said. "Some have even died for His sake."

Mitch stood up, shouting. "So is that it, then?" he demanded. "You think you'll win if you die? That's the kind of stupid remark I might have expected from your kind! Have you got any idea, lady, how many children have no mothers and fathers because their parents chose God over their own flesh and blood? You think that's noble or something? It's not. It's just brainwashing, pure and simple!" Mitch was panting now, his face very red and the veins in his neck throbbing.

A long moment passed as Helen waited for Mitch's anger to soften. Finally she spoke, in a voice so low he could hardly hear her. "Is that what you told your father?" she asked.

The words hung in the air like a secret that had been kept too long. Now it was Helen's turn to reach out and take hold of Mitch's hand. "How could you think I wouldn't know?" she asked earnestly. "It was only the biggest trial of our time—up until mine, that is. The first One Nation Earth world-justice prosecution. The first of Macalousso's show trials. Your father was one of us, the first of the martyrs for our cause."

Mitch had a stunned look on his face and the color drained away as he sat down, his knees suddenly weak. "All he had to do was say he didn't believe," he muttered, living his terrible memory for the thousandth time. "All he had to do was say three or four little words and he'd be here with us today. But he couldn't, could he?" Mitch's voice, trembling, began to rise again. "Once you high-and-mighty

Christians get it in your heads that you're on a mission from God, doing His divine will, there's no reason, no logic that will change your minds! It's madness!"

"Madness?" Helen echoed. "Is it madness to believe that there is a truth, a reality, beyond anything we can know? God is real, Mitch. And if you hadn't taken that mark on your hand, you'd know what I'm talking about."

Mitch angrily yanked his hand away and shoved it under his client's nose. "You think you've got all the answers?" he demanded. "You think you have some special ability to know what is true and what isn't? Well, you don't. I'm not the one who's blind to the truth, Helen. You are!"

Before her astonished eyes, he peeled back the 666 mark on his hand, revealing beneath the plastic overlay the tiny microchip that allowed him to pass for a loyal citizen of Macalousso's new world.

At the same, in the surveillance room beneath them, the two agents continued to troubleshoot their monitoring equipment. One poked his head out from beneath the console and muttered between tight lips, "If you think you can do better, Shearer, than why don't you get down here with me?"

Shearer shook his head. "I didn't say that, Catona," he replied. "All I said was that it's not working and that means we're going to have to fill out a report. And that means we're going to be here the rest of the day doing the paperwork." Shaking his head in utter frustration, he picked up the phone and violently punched a series of numbers.

Unwatched by her captors, Helen could only stare astonished at Mitch and the empty spot on his hand where the dreaded mark had once been. She looked up at him, her eyes full of unspoken questions.

"It's a black-market job," Mitch told her by way of explanation. "It fools the ONE mark detectors every time."

A stunned Helen was almost afraid to ask the next question. "So," she said hesitantly, "does that mean that . . . you're a Christian?"

Mitch's derisive laugh was the only answer she needed. "Let me tell you something, Helen," he said. "I believe in one thing and one thing only: Mitch Kendrick. Period. You'll never catch me following some miracle-working sorcerer from two thousand years ago. And I can guarantee you that He's not waiting for any of us on the other side of the grave. There's no big, white-bearded father waiting in open arms in heaven. That's all a never-neverland made up by people like you who are too frightened of real life to get by without some magical power on their side."

Helen open her mouth to protest, but Mitch cut her off with a savage gesture. "Don't give me all that claptrap about an afterlife, either," he continued. "I don't need the crutch my father used to make his life meaningful. I know first-hand what that can lead to. No way am I going to risk my neck for some pie-in-the-sky God who only turns His back on the suffering of this world. That's the same God who forced my father to abandon his son and give up his life for a fantasy of heaven. I'm not about to swallow that lie." He pressed the 666 patch back over the microchip on his hand and glared at Helen defiantly.

"I don't blame you for being bitter," Helen replied gently. "But you've got to believe that God doesn't abandon any of us. He's here right now. With both of us."

"Let's see how sure you are of that after this trial is over," Mitch answered curtly.

"But . . . but, " stammered the confused Helen, "I thought you were on our side. You said you wanted to put God on trial. You've got to do your best to defend your client. Even if you don't believe in His existence."

"Don't you get it?" asked Mitch with barely disguised contempt. "This whole thing has been a setup from the very beginning."

A long moment passed as Helen searched Mitch's eyes. "Maybe I'm wrong," she said at last. "But I think there's some good in you, Mitch Kendrick. I can't believe you'd compromise your professional ethics in a rigged trial, no matter what reward they dangled in front of you."

"Then you don't know Victoria Thorne," Mitch retorted, trying to ignore the pang of conscience that Helen's words had provoked. "She can be very persuasive. And very vindictive. She was the one who picked my father, out of thousands of Haters that ONE had in custody, and railroaded him in a show trial, just the way she's railroading you."

"But how?" Helen asked. "How could she get to you so easily?"

"There's nothing easy about it!" Mitch snapped back. "It's a matter of life and death. See, Ms. Hannah, my respected opponent in that courtroom knows all about my little deception." He held up his hand where the mark was now firmly back in place. "She used it to blackmail me into participating in my own father's trial. And she's using it to rope me into this one as well."

Helen shook her head, her eyes flashing defiant sparks. "You can't run from her forever, Mitch," she challenged him.

"Maybe not," he replied, and she heard the note of sadness and resignation in his voice. "But in this world there aren't a lot of places to hide. You do what you have to do to survive."

At that moment the door swung wide and Officers Shearer and Cantona rushed in. With a single smooth motion, Mitch snatched up the jamming device and dropped it into his briefcase before either of the surveillance agents caught a glimpse of it. He smiled in the face of their threatening scowls and Helen couldn't help but admire how finely tuned the lawyer's survival skills had become.

As the pair were searching the holding cell for the source of the static and interference on their monitors, another guard entered the room. "It's cleared up," he announced. "You guys better get back to your posts."

"I told you I'd get to the bottom of it," said Cantona with a hint of uncertainty as they crossed the room.

The guard signaled to Helen that her trial was about to get under way again.

∾

The second day of the trial began in an atmosphere tense with hatred and treachery. "Prosecution," the judge's voice boomed out over the packed courtroom, "you may call your first witness."

The gallery fell silent as Victoria moved from behind her table to the front of court, giving the impassive Helen and her lawyer, who could not hide the worried look on his face, a brief, contemptuous glance as she passed.

"I call to the stand General Tyson Kennan," Victoria announced, "commander in chief of the One Nation Earth Peace Corps."

Along with every eye in the courtroom, the television cameras directed their unblinking gaze to the middle-aged man in the crisp, heavily decorated uniform who moved down the aisle with an unassailable air of authority. Taking his seat in the witness stand, General Kennan raised his right hand as the bailiff approached.

"Do you swear to tell the truth, the whole truth, and nothing but the truth for the unity of the people of One Nation Earth?" asked the court officer, holding out a scroll of the ONE Constitution.

"I do," replied the general, placing his hand in the scroll.

The formalities dispensed with, Victoria wasted no time

laying out her plan of attack. "General Kennan," she asked in a probing tone, "as head of the ONE Peace Corps, how would you characterize the defining ethical and social beliefs of this planet prior to the arrival of Franco Macalousso and the establishment of his one-world government?"

"It was the so-called Christian era," replied the gruff military man with a contemptuous sneer.

"And what were the prevailing conditions during this era?" Victoria continued.

"Everything was fine," replied the general, drawing a surprised murmur from the crowd until he continued, "that is, if you don't count the prejudice and hatred. The genocide and ethnic cleansing. The widespread starvation and poverty." He shook his head with disgust at the memory. "In short, Ms. Thorne, it was hell. A living hell."

Victoria nodded sympathetically. "There are many of us here today who have tried to forget the horror and despair of those times," she remarked. "But as I'm sure you'll agree, it's important to keep such memories alive, if only as a warning to future generations. Perhaps, General Kennan, you would agree to recount for us some of the more graphic examples of the hell on earth you describe."

Kennan began to count off the examples on the fingers of his hands. "As I'm sure you know, Ms. Thorne," he said, "in the twentieth century alone, we suffered through World War I and II, Korea, Vietnam, Bosnia—and those were only the large-scale conflicts that were reported in the media. Everywhere across the planet, on a daily and even hourly basis, there were examples of barbaric cruelty and murderous prejudice in daily life. Violence, suffering, destruction, and despair: these were our constant companions."

Victoria pursed her lips and shook her head as if the recollections of those dark ages were too much to bear. She let a moment pass in silence before continuing her questioning. "Terrible times, indeed, General," she said at last. "But we live in a new age today. Perhaps you could tell us what are the challenges faced by you, the commander of the Peace Corps, since the establishment of One Nation Earth by Franco Macalousso."

"Well," the general answered, his face breaking into a craggy grin, "we've had to organize some pretty substantial celebrations. In fact, our job these days is mostly to make sure that people have full access to the events that have the institution of this new age: parties, festivals, block parties. Folks seem to be in the mood to have a good time."

Laughter and cheers greeted the general's words from the gallery and Victoria paused to let the happy shouts subside. "So," she continued after a moment, "would it be fair to say that while the Christians' so-called Lord brought suffering and death, Franco Macalousso and One Nation Earth have ushered in an era of peace and plenty unknown in human history?"

"The remarkable thing," added General Kennan, "is that it all happened so quickly. Practically overnight! We went from poverty to plenty in record time, and I don't think I'd get any disagreement if I said that the world and its people have never been in better shape."

More shouts and cheering interrupted the general's testimony and Judge Wells indulgently let them continue for several minutes before banging his gavel for order.

"I take it you would agree," Victoria responded, "that the arrival of Franco Macalousso was a turning point in the battle of the human race to achieve equality, justice, and peace."

"I wouldn't agree," countered the general, and once again a gasp was heard from the gallery. "I would say that it was the beginning. Before our messiah mankind was groaning under the accumulated weight of superstition and suffering. We have been released to realize our full potential for the first time. This is not a turning point in our history, Ms. Thorne. It is the beginning of our history. From this point forward we are living in a new world."

"A world, in your opinion as a career military man, brought about by the wisdom, guidance, and leadership abilities of Franco Macalousso?" asked Victoria with a triumphant turn to the cameras.

"No one else could have accomplished such an amazing transformation in so short a time," replied the general enthusiastically.

"No more questions, Your Honor," the prosecutor said as she returned to her table.

The courtroom broke out in spontaneous applause.

Helen leaned over and whispered into her lawyer's ear. "Ask him what price we've paid," she urged Mitch.

"What?" Mitch replied. "What are you talking about?"

"I'm talking about the lessons of history," Helen shot back. "The Nazis brought peace too. But look what they demanded of the people for it."

"You expect me to bring that up here?" he demanded as he eyed the judge, who was waiting impatiently for the cross-examination. "Nobody is interested in history. It's the future we're talking about."

Mitch stood up. "No questions at this time, Your Honor," he announced.

"What are you doing?" demanded an angry Helen as he sat back down. "You've got to challenge him!"

"With what?" Mitch demanded to know. "Some ancient history about Nazis? You expect me to object to testimony that Franco Macalousso is the savior of mankind? Get real, lady."

"You may call your next witness, Madame Prosecutor," Judge Wells announced, nodding toward Victoria.

"Very well, Your Honor," she replied, standing again. "At this time I would like to call to the stand Mr. William Spino."

As a wiry man made his way to the stand with a cocky stride, Mitch turned with a puzzled look to his client. "Who's this guy?" he asked.

Helen swallowed hard. "He's . . . my brother," she said, sadness and dismay coloring her words.

Chapter 9

"WHEN MY BROTHER TOOK THE MARK he changed," Helen whispered to her lawyer, her eyes bright with tears. "We used to be so close. But I lost him . . . forever. It's as if they sucked out his soul and left an empty shell."

As the bailiff finished swearing in Willie Spino with the scroll of the ONE Constitution, Willie stared happily around the courtroom, obviously delighted at being the center of attention for the entire world. As the cameras zoomed in for their obligatory tight shot, Victoria rose and stopped Helen's brother before he could sit in the witness chair.

"Mr. Spino," she said, "I wonder if I might prevail upon you for a little demonstration before we begin our testimony." She turned to Judge Wells. "With the court's permission?" she asked.

"Proceed," replied the judge brusquely.

"Sure thing, Sweetheart," said Willie, catching the drift of her strategy and, still grinning broadly, walked with a spring in his step to the defense table and back.

"Thank you, Mr. Spino," Victoria responded. "You may

take your seat now." She turned to the cameras as Helen's brother settled into the witness stand. "Six months ago, ladies and gentlemen, the man you see before you would have been utterly unable to complete the simple exercise you just witnessed." She turned back to Willie. "Isn't that so, Mr. Spino?"

"You got that right, ma'am," he replied and a ripple of laughter rolled through the courtroom. The witness was obviously making the most out of his moment in the spotlight. "I was a helpless cripple back then."

"A helpless cripple," Victoria repeated for dramatic effect. "Is it correct to say that you couldn't have walked or even crawled into this courtroom today in your former condition?"

"I could have rolled in," Willie volunteered. "You see, I was confined to a wheelchair." More laughter greeted his words. It was hard to tell who was getting a bigger kick out of the proceedings—Willie or the audience.

"May I ask you," Victoria continued after the laughter had subsided, "how it is that you managed to regain the use of your legs?"

"You surely can," enthused Willie Spino. "It was Franco Macalousso, the messiah. He is the one who made me walk again." He looked around the room, beaming with joy, as if inviting the whole world to join in his admiration.

"And how exactly did he accomplish this amazing feat, Mr. Spino?" asked Victoria as she led the willing witness exactly where she wanted him to go.

"He told me to believe in him and believe in his promises," Willie replied. "It was as simple as that."

"And those promises made by Mr. Macalousso," Victoria pressed. "Did he tell you anything else you'd like to share with the court today? Anything you'd like to tell us about?"

Willie's grin grew even wider. "I think showing might be better than just telling," he replied. Turning to Judge Wells, he asked, "Do you mind, Your Honor?"

"Go right ahead, Mr. Spino," Judge Wells answered benevolently.

Willie closed his eyes for a moment and when he opened them again, he pointed suddenly and deliberately at a pitcher of water that sat in front of Helen on the defense table. The pitcher began to tremble and shake and then, with a sudden swift motion, flew off the table and spilled into Helen's lap.

The court erupted into raucous laughter, loud shouts of approval, and catcalls of ridicule for the soaked defendant.

"Very impressive, Mr. Spino," Victoria continued, having more than a little trouble keeping her own self-satisfied smile under control. "But of course, you are hardly alone in demonstrating these remarkable abilities, are you now?"

Willie scoffed. "Of course not, ma'am," he replied. "Franco Macalousso can teach anyone to unleash his hidden powers. He's done it for millions—billions, I dare say."

Victoria nodded. This was more like it. Unlike the unpleasant surprises of yesterday, today's session was running like clockwork. "To continue, Mr. Spino," she said, "can you tell the court how it is that you know the defendant, Ms. Helen Hannah?"

"She's my half-sister," replied Willie, his nose wrinkling with obvious distaste.

"And tell me, Mr. Spino," Victoria continued, ready with her next barbed question. "Was your half-sister happy to see you healed and free from your confinement in a wheelchair?"

"Objection," interjected Mitch, rising from his seat. "Calls for speculation on the witness's part."

"Sustained," remarked Judge Wells grudgingly, throwing a angry look at the defense lawyer. This was no time to stray from their careful plans.

"Well, then," Victoria pressed on, rephrasing her question. "Tell us how Helen Hannah responded when she saw the amazing change in you, Mr. Spino."

"She said it was evil," Willie answered in a low, ominous tone. "She said she wished I'd stayed a cripple, that I had disobeyed her God by turning to Mr. Macalousso." His voice rose to a shrill pitch. "But her God never did a thing for me except give me two legs that didn't work!" He pointed at Helen. "Ask her how come God made me a cripple! Ask her!"

"I have no further questions, Your Honor," Victoria concluded triumphantly as she returned to the prosecution's desk.

"Does the defense wish to cross-examine?" the judge asked Mitch.

"Ask him what price he had to pay," Helen urgently whispered in his ear.

"Look," he said, turning to her and scolding her with a

harsh undertone. "Will you please let me handle this my way?"

"Counselor," the judge repeated crossly, "will you or will you not be cross-examining the witness?"

Mitch took a deep breath and stood up. "Yes, Your Honor," he said.

In the next second a furious look passed between Wells, Mitch, and Victoria. All three knew that the defense attorney was breaking the rules. A cross-examination hadn't been scripted. Mitch was out on his own again, taking risks with their carefully orchestrated game plan. But with the eyes of the world turned on them, there was nothing for Judge Wells and Victoria to do but let Mitch have his way.

"Very well, Counselor," the judge growled. "You may proceed."

Mitch rose and approached the witness stand where Willie sat with a startled look. He hadn't been coached for a cross-examination.

"Mr. Spino," Mitch began, "your testimony, and your demonstration, are certainly remarkable. Would you say that you are an example of the good things that Franco Macalousso has brought to our world?"

"More than an example," replied Willie proudly. "I'm a living poster boy."

"A poster boy," Mitch repeated. "That's a good way to put it. He's healed your body and bestowed amazing mental powers on you in the bargain."

"I'm not just taller," Willie cracked. "I'm also sharper."

Guffaws greeted his words. The gallery was enjoying the show immensely.

"Sharp and tall," Mitch repeated, as if musing on the phrase. "I guess you could say the whole world is a sharper and taller since Mr. Macalousso came on the scene. Mass healing. Newly realized human potential on a worldwide scale. You can't argue with success, can you, Mr. Spino?"

"No, you can't," Willie agreed, narrowing his eyes as if he sensed a trap being set.

Mitch strolled back to the defense table and was about to sit down when a thought seemed to occur to him. He turned, just as the judge and Victoria were exchanging a pleased look, and cleared his throat. "Oh," he said, "just one more question, Mr. Spino, if you don't mind."

Willie, who was halfway out of his seat, froze and looked helplessly at the judge.

Wells gestured for him to sit back down. "Make it brief, Mr. Kendrick," the judge ordered.

"Of course, Your Honor," Mitch replied amicably. "I was just wondering how the witness feels about his sister here."

"What do you mean?" Willie replied, his suspicions growing.

"Would you say that you love her?" Mitch asked innocently.

"Love?" Willie replied, casting another desperate look, this time at Victoria. "I wouldn't call it love."

"What would you call it?" Mitch pressed.

"I'd call it hate!" spat Willie vehemently. "How would you feel if your sister treated you the way Helen treated me?"

"Well," replied Mitch, "that's an interesting question. I guess it would depend on when you asked me."

"I don't follow," said the bewildered Willie.

"Let me put it this way," Mitch continued, moving closer. "Before you took the mark on your hand, before your sister was branded an outlaw and a criminal—did you love her then?"

Willie looked mystified and Victoria, who had been watching the proceedings like a hawk, realized a moment too late that the trap had been sprung.

"Answer the question, Mr. Spino," Mitch insisted.

"Your Honor—" Victoria began, rising to her feet.

"Of course I loved her," Willie let out. "She was my sister, after all."

"Objection!" shouted Helen. "That's totally irrelevant!"

"Sustained!" boomed Judge Wells and turned to Mitch, shaking his gavel at him. "You are completely out of line, Mr. Kendrick!"

"No further questions, Your Honor," Mitch said, and as he turned to face the defense table, he winked broadly at Helen.

"Court is adjourned for one hour," huffed Judge Wells. "Counsel," he commanded, "in my chambers. Now."

⌘

Ten minutes later, Mitch stood like a chastened schoolboy in the judge's oak-paneled study, listening to a fierce tongue-lashing as he secretly relished the annoyance he was causing the judge and his opponent by throwing a wrench into their carefully constructed machinery.

Finally, after Judge Wells paused long enough to catch his breath, Mitch managed to get a word in edgewise. "I don't know what you expected," he protested. "I thought you said you wanted this trial to look and sound like the real thing. I'm just trying to give some authenticity to this circus. I'm sure that's what Franco Macalousso would want."

"You call that authenticity?" seethed Victoria. "All you were doing was trying to trap that witness. To make him look foolish by playing on his emotions."

"I just ask the questions," Mitch shrugged, trying hard to hide his smile. "How the witness looks by answering them isn't my problem. All he had to do was say he loved his sister. It was a slam dunk. But this guy couldn't keep his foot out of his mouth." He shook his head ruefully as he turned to Victoria. "Don't you believe in coaching your witnesses?"

"He was coached!" she replied angrily. "He was coached not to expect a cross-examination from you."

"Enough!" interjected Judge Wells in his sternest tone of voice. He looked at Mitch. "Young man," he continued, "I want no more antics from you. Is that understood?"

"No problem," replied Mitch as he crossed to the door. "From now on I'll just hold up cue cards so that the prosecution will know what part of the trial we're in." He glanced over his shoulder at Victoria. "Hate for you to fall behind in the play-by-play."

Chapter 10

SELMA AND SHERRI SAT NEXT to the Goss brothers at a broken-down kitchen table they had salvaged from a condemned building and dragged to their abandoned subway station hideout. Before them were maps and charts of the city and its environs, and the outlaw believers studied them carefully, combing the urban jungle as they looked for clues to their next move.

Behind them a bell rang, triggered by a trip wire at the entrance to the boarded-up station. The alarm caused them all to dive for cover, with Jake grabbing a gun from his belt and crouching low to cover the others.

"Relax, everyone," said a familiar voice from the shadows at the top of the stairs. "It's just me."

"J. T.!" cried the excited Sherri and she bolted from behind a pile of debris to meet her husband. She threw her arms around him and covered his grimy face with kisses. He reached out to stroke her cheek, and it was at that moment that she noticed the mark of 666 on his hand. With a stifled cry she stepped back, horrified.

"Don't worry, sweetheart," J. T. said with a reassuring smile. "It's not real."

"You think we'd be with him if it was?" came a voice from behind him as Dawn and Dave stepped into the dim light of the hideout. As J. T. made the introductions, the two fugitives looked cautiously around them, uncertain if the rebel believers would accept them into their fold.

"They're friends of mine from way back," J. T. explained. "I met up with them in the old neighborhood."

"Are they . . . with us?" asked Sherri uncertainly.

"We're not Christians, if that's what you mean," replied Dawn. "But we can help you get your friend out of jail, if that means anything to you."

Selma gave J. T. a dubious look. "So now we're using the unsaved to do our dirty work for us?" she asked, folding her arms across her chest.

"I trust them," J. T. replied evenly. "I'll vouch for them."

Selma shook her head. "Your vouching for them doesn't mean a thing if they get caught and are forced to take the mark. They could betray us, destroy everything we're trying to accomplish."

J. T. put his arm around her. "Don't worry so much, Sel," he advised. "They can handle themselves as well as any of us. Dawn knows security systems backward and forward and Dave used to have a job in the court. We've already worked up a good plan."

He pulled away and turned to face the others. "But that's not all. Dawn here has some information I think you'll all be real interested in." J. T. looked over to her. "Tell them what you told me," he urged.

Dawn shrugged. "It's just that I was with that lawyer who's defending your friend. He pretends to be one of them, but he's not. His mark—it's fake. I got a good look and I'm sure of it."

The Goss brothers and Selma, J. T., and Sherri all looked at each other. The expression they shared said it all. *A fake mark. Maybe that's why Helen seems to be putting so much trust and confidence in her lawyer.*

Helen was dozing as she sat in her holding-cell chair, her thoughts blending seamlessly with her dreams as she imagined herself in another place, a better place, far from the terrors and intimidation that had haunted her life ever since she first heard the name of Franco Macalousso. It was a beautiful place, warm and inviting, full of light and shimmering with the presence of God. She could have lingered there forever, leaving her body behind and letting her spirit float free to return to its Maker and the paradise He had prepared for her.

The slamming of the cell door woke her from her reverie and she opened her eyes to see Mitch Kendrick, holding a finger over his lips as he activated the scrambler and set it on the table.

Far below them in the surveillance room, Officers Cantona and Shearer were completely oblivious to the static that was now interrupting the transmission from Helen's holding cell. Instead, they were both fully engrossed in another monitor on the far side of the room showing two attractive ONE agents getting undressed in the ladies' locker room of the courthouse security wing.

"Think about it, Helen," Mitch was saying as his client tried to clear her head of the last vestiges of her beautiful vision. "You can't really expect me to equate the accomplishments of Franco Macalousso with the regime of the Nazis. We're trying to win sympathy for you, not spur on a lynch mob." He leaned over the table, fixing her with an intent gaze. "Maybe there's something you don't quite understand. My life is on the line here too. I need to be very, very careful and the last thing I can start spouting off about is eternal souls, salvation, and all the rest of those fairy tales my father was always talking about. I need evidence, hard evidence."

Helen returned his stare. "Just because you can't see something, Mitch," she told him, "doesn't mean it doesn't exist."

Mitch sighed with impatience. "Just what is that supposed to mean?" he asked.

"Think about it," she urged him. "You believe in joy and truth, don't you? And you can see them. How about gravity? If it weren't for that invisible reality we'd all be floating around in outer space. The Bible says that 'faith is the substance of things hoped for, the evidence of things not seen.'"

"There you go again," he huffed, throwing up his arms, "always spiritualizing everything."

Helen couldn't help but smile. "Okay, Mitch," she said, "let's try another approach. Do you believe in love?"

"Of course," he replied. "I loved my dad, if that's what you mean."

"Where's your proof?" Helen challenged. "How do you know it exists?"

Mitch opened his mouth but nothing came out. He broke off his gaze and paced to a far corner of the room. "I don't have time for this," he grumbled.

"Is it the time you lack, Mitch," Helen wanted to know, "or is it the will?" Her voice reached out to him, pleading for his spirit to hear and respond. "The answers are right in front of you. Don't be afraid to open your eyes and look."

Mitch was silent for a long minute and Helen was beginning to think that just maybe she was starting to get through to him when he turned with a vehement look on his face.

"And what about you?" he asked. "What are the answers for you, all alone here in this cell, with the whole world against you? Don't tell me you're not frightened. Don't tell me you wouldn't give anything to be out of this place, away from this danger. You want safety and security as much as the next person and if you say you don't, you're just lying."

Helen's face dropped. She put her head in her hands. "Of course I do," she sighed. "I'm just a human being,

Mitch. Flesh and blood, like anyone else. Naturally I'm scared. Who wouldn't be? I'm the first one to admit that I'm not as strong as I should be . . . as He wants me to be." Her voice trailed off and, in that instant, Mitch regretted his harsh words.

"Hey look," he said as he moved closer and put his arm across her shoulder. "I'm sorry. I had no right."

"You had every right," Helen said with conviction, looking up at him with tears welling in her eyes. "I expect you to have the courage to face what you don't understand and here I am, just as terrified as you are of the unknown." Her voice trembled. "I am terrified, Mitch. I don't want to die. I'm sorry if that disappoints you."

Mitch smiled comfortingly. "I'm not disappointed," he reassured her. "Believe me. I know exactly where you're coming from."

Helen shook her head. "I only wish you did," she countered. "You called your father's faith a crutch. But let me ask you: what's easier? To follow the rest of the world because you're afraid to go against what everyone says is right or to stand up for God, even if your voice is the only one?" She laughed, but Mitch could hear the choking sob behind it. "If that's a crutch, then it's not a very study one. Do you think I get any satisfaction from being hated by the whole world? Where's the security and safety in that?"

"Not everyone hates you," Mitch said and a new note of gentleness and compassion had entered his voice.

"Don't try and make me feel better, Counselor," Helen

replied. "You called me a mindless puppet out there. Is that the kind of person you could love—or even like?"

"Helen, I—" Mitch began, but she silenced him with a wave of her hand.

"I may be a believer," she continued adamantly, "but I'm still a human being too. I struggle with fears and doubts just as anyone else does. Are my feelings any less real than those of all the people who are pledging allegiance to Franco Macalousso? What about my brother, Mitch? When you asked him if he loved me, what did you expect him to say?"

"I . . . honestly didn't know," the lawyer admitted.

Helen wiped away the tears that spilled down her cheeks. "It was the right thing to ask," she asserted. "Love is something that Macalousso and his followers are doing their best to eradicate from the face of the earth. It's something we've got to hold onto." She took him by the hand. "It's something we've got to believe in."

༄

In their subterranean hideout, the ragged band of believers were having a hard time accepting J. T.'s unorthodox introduction of two non-Christian renegades into their ranks The Goss brothers simply looked at each other and shook their heads, while Selma and Sherri exchanged worried looks.

"Let me get this straight," said Tony at last. "You guys aren't believers, but you're going to help us with this dangerous and potentially lethal mission anyway."

"I promised them the mark-detector jammers," J. T. explained.

"Plus food," Dave reminded him. "Don't forget about the food."

Sherri stepped forward. "We'll give you something to eat whether you help us or not," she said kindly. "We just can't afford to have anything go wrong."

"We've got that covered," replied J. T. with a knowing smile. "Show him, Dave."

The grubby, hungry young man reached behind him and produced a suitcase he had set on the stairs. Opening it, he displayed a virtually armory of firepower, from handguns to fully automatic assault weapons.

Tony let out a low whistle and shared an impressed look with his brother. Selma and Sherri felt the same apprehensive shudder race down their spines.

◌◌

It was impossible to tell how much time had passed since Mitch and Helen had begun their intense, sometimes angry conversation in the holding cell. There were no clocks on the wall, no windows to reflect the passing of the day. They could have been together for only a few hours or kept a vigil throughout the long night.

For Helen, it no longer mattered. Ever since she had been held a prisoner, time had ceased to exist. It was as if eternity were drawing ever closer.

For Mitch, on the other hand, each passing minute was

agony. If he couldn't convince his client to cooperate with him, there was no way he could help her. And without help, she was surely going to be put to death. Somehow, over the course of the past few days, he had come to care very much about her fate.

"Do you mind telling me something?" Mitch asked Helen as beyond the barred door, they could hear the slow footsteps of the guards, changing duty for the day. "If it's so painful knowing you're hated this way, if you're as scared of death as anyone else, then why, in the name of this God you worship, why don't you just give them what they want? Take the mark! Join the rest of the world! Pledge your loyalty to Franco Macalousso. You may not have won the war, but at least you will have survived."

"Try to see it from my point of view," Helen pleaded. "They want me to deny Jesus, my Savior. But Jesus is the only reason I have for trying to stay alive. He's the only thing keeping me sane."

Mitch clenched his first in sheer frustration. "That's exactly the kind of thing I might have expected you to say," he remarked through gritted teeth. "It's exactly the same kind of insanity that killed my father."

"It's the truth," Helen said softly, but with complete conviction. "It's not as if I, or your father, just decided we wanted it to be true. It just is. And that leaves us no choice."

Now it was Mitch's turn to plead. "How can I help you if you won't help yourself, Helen?" he asked. "How can I defend you if you choose to believe something that will cost you your life?"

Helen looked at him, her eyes growing wide. "Let me testify," she said at last, in a voice so low he could hardly hear her. "Put me on the stand."

A involuntary jolt of fear raced through Mitch's body. His face dropped, but he did his best to hide what was he was feeling from his client. "That's impossible," he said, with as much finality as he could muster. "Victoria would take you apart up there on cross-examination. Besides, I thought you were frightened to face a world so hostile to you and what you believe."

"Of course I'm frightened," Helen replied promptly. "But it's my only chance." She reached across the table and took hold of Mitch's hands in her own. "I'll make a deal with you, Mr. Counselor," she said, fixing him with her eyes. "I'll give you a piece of information that will make Victoria Thorne wish she had never stepped foot in that courtroom or heard the name Helen Hannah. In exchange, you give me my chance in the witness stand." She paused, searching his eyes. "Deal?"

The cell door swung open and a beefy guard entered. "They want you back in court, Hater," he said with contempt, then nodded to Mitch. "You too, lawyer boy."

As they rose, Mitch leaned over and whispered into Helen's ear, "Get me what I need," he said, his voice trembling with uncertainty, "and I'll see what I can do."

Chapter 11

YOU'VE GOT TO BE KIDDING!" Sherri's voice, ringing with disbelief, echoed through the dusty tile walls of the deserted subway station. She was staring at the open suitcase Dave held out in front of him, packed with guns of every description—enough deadly firepower, it seemed to her, to take on half the ONE security force.

"I've never been more serious in my life," J. T. replied earnestly to his young wife. "Sherri, if those 666ers are so bound and determined to get a one-way pass into hell, then why shouldn't we help them out a little?" He grinned. "It's only the neighborly thing to do."

Selma gave him a skeptical look, crossing her arms and arching her eyebrows. "Let me get something straight," she said. "That mark you have on your hand—you're sure it's fake, right? I mean, are you one of us or not?"

In answer to her question, J. T. walked over to Dave and pulled a particularly nasty piece of hardware out of the suitcase. "If you do that which is evil," he said, paraphrasing the

Bible as he brandished the gun, "be afraid; for he bears not the sword in vain."

"You can't take that out of context," protested Sherri. "Scripture doesn't tell us to go around shooting our enemies. 'Thou shalt not kill.' Remember that one, J. T.? It's one of the Ten Commandments, in case you've forgotten."

"Amen," agreed Selma fervently. "You go out with guns blazing like some desperado, you're only going to prove what Macalousso has been saying about us all along."

J. T. shook his head adamantly. "No," he countered, the word sounding harsh in their dimly lighted hideout. "What I'd be proving is that God's might is greater than any adversary's. Maybe, if we really want to beat the devil, we've got to use a little firepower ourselves. I heard it said once that all it takes for evil to prosper is for good people to do nothing. I don't know about the rest of you, but I'm tired of doing nothing."

Selma reached out and put a soothing hand on J. T.'s muscled arm. "I know how you feel, J. T.," she said. "But think about the implications of what you're suggesting. We have a responsibility before God—to be a light for the rest of the world to see."

J. T. could only shake his head sadly. "You just don't get, it do you?" He looked around at the others. "None of you gets it. Who's going to be a light for the world after Macalousso gets finished hunting us all down and killing us, one by one, just as he's doing to Helen?"

"Do you think you're going to change people's minds with that thing on your hand?" Sherri challenged, pointing to mark imprinted into his flesh.

"Sherri, please," he replied. "It's just a fake. It doesn't mean anything. I've got to have the ability to move freely and not be noticed. It's the only way I've got a chance of saving Helen."

Sherri shook her head stubbornly. "It still stands for everything evil in this world," she insisted. "It's like a brand that says you're owned by the enemy."

"You know what's in my heart, Sherri," J. T. responded, looking deep into her eyes. "What's on my hand doesn't matter."

As Sherri struggled to understand her feelings, Dave and Dawn moved to a table near the television monitors and began busily eating from the rations that were piled on it. "Hey," said Dave, his mouth full of crackers and cheese. "The trial's back on."

Their differences forgotten for the moment, the others gathered around the screen as the now-familiar image of the courtroom came into view.

"All rise," the bailiff intoned as Judge Wells entered from a side door. Wasting no time, he instructed Victoria to call her first witness of the session.

"One Nation Earth calls Helen Hannah," said Victoria and waited for the excitement that greeted her surprise announcement to die away.

"Objection," Mitch interjected, rising to his feet. "The prosecution knows full well that it may not call the defendant as a witness in her own trial."

"Overruled," snapped Judge Wells.

"But, Your Honor—" Mitch began.

The judge cut him off with a heavy bang from his gavel. "Counsel is apparently not aware," he said with contempt, "of the newly revised statute enacted in the recent legislative session under the guidance of Franco Macalousso."

"Well, uh . . . actually—" Mitch stuttered.

"Your Honor," Victoria interrupted impatiently, "if I had know that part of our purpose here today was to educate the defense on all of the most current legal developments, I would have brought my law library for him to study."

A ripple of laughter spread through the court as Mitch's face reddened.

"I repeat," Victoria continued firmly, "I call to the stand Helen Hannah."

Her lawyer was about to lodge yet another protest when Helen stopped him with a gentle touch. "God may be opening a door here," she whispered to Mitch. "Just make sure in cross-examination that you ask me about what I believe."

Standing up and moving toward the witness stand, Helen felt the eyes of the entire world pinning her down like an insect on a tray. This was her moment and she offered a silent but heartfelt prayer for strength and guidance from God.

"Do you swear to tell the truth, the whole truth, and nothing but the truth for the unity of the people of One Nation Earth?" the bailiff intoned, as he held up the ONE Constitution scroll.

"Not based on that document," Helen countered. "But I do promise to tell the truth, as God is my witness." She raised her right hand.

The bailiff looked expectantly to Judge Wells, who in turn directed a questioning glance at Victoria Thorne. A silent moment passed.

"The prosecution has no particular objection," the prosecutor responded at last. "If the witness believes that such a vow will compel her to be honest, we will accept it for purposes of gaining her testimony."

"I'll allow it," said the judge. "You may proceed."

Helen repeated the vow in a low voice, her inflection rising as she reached the words, "and nothing but the truth, so help me God." She took her seat in the witness stand.

Victoria approached with all the stealth of a cat toying with a captive rodent. "Ms. Hannah," she began, "is it true that you believe our great leader and messiah, Franco Macalousso, is in fact an evil tyrant bent on enslaving the world?"

Helen opened her mouth to answer but Victoria continued relentlessly. "Is it also true that you believe that anyone and everyone who follows him is deluded and damned to eternal punishment in the fires of hell?"

"I never said that," Helen asserted. "Franco Macalousso

and his followers will be judged by their own words. Not by mine."

"So," Victoria pressed on, "what you're saying to us here today is that while the rest of humanity is solidly behind the achievements and vision of our great leader, you believe that we are all, to use the metaphor with which I began this trial, paddling straight into a deadly whirlpool. That we are all wrong and you alone know the truth?"

"Not just I," replied Helen softly. "There are others."

"There may be others," Victoria countered, "but you are the one who's on trial here today, Ms. Hannah. Please answer the question."

"My answer is no," Helen stated, clearly and unequivocally. "Those statements to do not reflect my true beliefs."

"We have evidence to the contrary!" Victoria shot back. "Must I remind you that you are under oath?"

"I'm not against peace and unity," Helen responded firmly. "I would love to see the day when we realize that we are all the same in God's eyes. But that will come only when we understand that our eternal hope is not in this world and never will be."

"So what you are saying," responded Victoria, leaning over the railing of the witness stand, "is that because you believe in a life beyond this one, you are willing to sacrifice the safety and harmony of the entire world just to prove that your antiquated faith in God is more than the worst sort of primitive superstition."

Helen looked deeply into Victoria's eyes, then turned to

confront Judge Wells's glare as a long moment elapsed. "I'm saying, Ms. Thorne," she replied at last, "that knowing God is worth any sacrifice."

Victoria turned triumphantly to face the cameras. "This God of yours," she crowed. "He must be a very impressive deity. I wonder what's He's like." She turned back to Helen. "Can you describe Him for us, Ms. Hannah?"

"No man has seen God and lived," Helen responded. "It is Jesus Christ alone who shows us the Father."

"So," the sly prosecutor continued, "I guess it's fair to say that you've never actually spoken to this great Father in the sky?"

"I read His words," the defendant replied, "in the Bible."

"I'm talking about personally," Victoria insisted. "Face-to-face. Up close and personal. The way you and I are speaking right now."

"Of course not," Helen retorted.

"And have you ever known anyone who has had such a conversation with the almighty Creator?"

"No," Helen admitted. "I haven't."

The lady prosecutor turned again to the camera and when she spoke, her voice dripped with sarcasm. "So," she intoned, "what you're telling this court is that you are willing to deprive the entire world of its sense of purpose and security, its very hope for the future, all for the sake of someone whom you've never seen or talked to and who has never said so much as a word to you. Is that it, Ms Hannah?"

Helen sat silently as around her the gallery erupted into derisive laughter and catcalls. When the tumult, unchecked by the judge, finally died down, Victoria continued, "Selfish. Deluded. Bigoted. Do you think that a fair description of how you've presented yourself here today, Ms. Hannah?"

Helen remained mute, absorbing the insults and hatred with a look of calm determination.

"No further questions, Your Honor," Victoria announced as she returned to the prosecution table with a self-satisfied smirk in Mitch's direction.

"Very well," replied Judge Wells. "If there is no cross-examination, the witness is asked to step down."

In the next moment, the world crawled at a snail's pace for Helen as she watched her lawyer struggle with his conscience. She registered the judge's stern look at Mitch, as if warning him against speaking out, and saw the pained expression that passed over the young attorney's face in turn. She sat in silent witness as Mitch turned to look at Victoria, who only nodded and pointed with her eyes to the figure of a sinister man, dressed all in black, watching the proceedings from the rear of the courtroom. The last thing Helen saw before she heard the judge speak again was the menacing stare and icy smile that this dark stranger directed toward Mitch. The meaning was only too clear: not only was Mitch's reputation in danger; his life was dangling by the decision he would make in the next few seconds.

"Very well," she heard Judge Wells announce. "You may step down, Ms. Hannah."

Victoria's grim expression turned condescending and Helen, feeling a crushing weight descend on her spirit, stood and stepped from the witness stand.

It was at that moment that Mitch, his head in his hands, sat bolt upright, as if he had experienced a sudden and powerful new insight. A light began to glow in his eyes and he stood up, his voice clear and penetrating in the far reaches of the courtroom. "Sorry, Your Honor," he announced, "but if it please the court, the defense will cross-examine."

Helen and her lawyer had barely a moment to exchange an exultant glance as Mitch moved to the witness stand and behind him the crowd began to mutter angrily.

Judge Wells and Victoria traded a look as well, one full of alarm and misgivings and the sure knowledge that it was too late to stop Mitch now, with the eyes of world turned on them.

"Keep it short, Counselor," the judge grumbled. "You've already wasted enough of the court's valuable time."

"Of course, Your Honor," Mitch replied and turned to Helen, a slight smile playing at the corners of his mouth. "Ms. Hannah," he began, glancing quickly at the scribbled notes on the pad in his hand. "Recalling this boat of our planet that the able prosecution has described so vividly— could you tell the court why you have refused to row along with everyone else? Why, Ms. Hannah, have you chosen to turn against what virtually everyone else on the boat under-stands to be the only way we will ever reach a safe harbor?"

Helen was silent for a moment as her thoughts raced to put words to the answer that was already forming in her mind. She took a deep breath and when she spoke, it was in a voice so low and intense that every spectator leaned for-ward in his chair to hear what she had to say. "Unity is important," she began earnestly, "believe me, I know that. We've all got to work together for the common good. But to put all our trust in that boat, to think that we can row our-selves out of harm's way without some help outside of our-selves, well . . . that's a lie and a delusion."

"Objection," interrupted Victoria shrilly, an edge of desperation in her voice. "Does the defendant expect the court to believe that she knows all and the rest of us are ignorant? Some of the greatest minds in the world have given their commitment and devoted their energy to the one-world government of Franco Macalousso."

"Sustained," intoned Judge Wells with authority. "You will confine your questions to matters of fact, Counselor," he added sternly, peering down at Mitch.

The lawyer sighed heavily and Helen could see the mounting frustration he felt as he was increasingly hemmed in by the prosecutor and the judge. There wasn't much room for maneuver and if Mitch was going to score points, he'd have to do it right under the noses of his opponents.

Thinking for a moment, the defense attorney turned back to his client. "Ms. Hannah," he said in a clear and forthright tone, "please answer this question to the best of your abilities: what is two plus two?"

Helen threw him a confused look. Where was he heading with this?

He nodded slightly, as if asking her to trust him.

"Four," she said. "Obviously."

"Obviously," Mitch echoed. "But what if the whole world said that two plus two equaled five, Ms. Hannah? Would the weight of their majority opinion make it so?"

"Of course not," Helen replied promptly, catching his drift. "It would still be four. The truth is the truth, even if only one person knows it."

"But," Mitch pressed, "what if the happiness and prosperity of the whole world depended on two plus two equaling five? Wouldn't that change the answer for you?"

"Objection!" Victoria shouted strenuously. She could see only too well where Mitch was taking his witness and knew it was imperative to cut him off as soon as possible. "Your Honor," she continued, flustered and stumbling over her words, "The witness is . . . not a . . . mathematics expert."

The absurdity of the statement sent a titter through the galleries. The judge looked at Victoria in surprise as if to ask if that was the best she could do. There was simply no way he could sustain that objection without looking as foolish as she did.

"Overruled," Judge Wells mumbled begrudgingly, and turned to Helen. "You may answer the question."

"It wouldn't matter if all the people in the world said it

was five," Helen answered as she threw Mitch a quick smile. "Not in the slightest. Number don't lie."

"Wait just a minute, Ms. Hannah," Mitch continued, his voice rising in mock outrage. "By making such a statement, aren't you just proving how prejudiced and narrow-minded your views really are? Why can't you simply compromise with the majority opinion? After all, the whole world would be so much happier if two plus two would equal five."

"There's no compromise with truth," Helen answered boldly. "It's either one thing or the other. It can't be both and it can't be neither."

"If I understand you correctly, then," Mitch concluded, leaning over the rail of the witness stand and fixing Helen with a searching gaze, "what you're telling this court here today is that the truth is absolute."

"Objection!" sputtered Victoria, her voice quaking with anger and a trace of fear. "The witness is not an expert on matters of truth."

"Sustained," snapped Judge Wells with relief. At least he could uphold her objection this time.

"I'll rephrase the question," said Mitch amicably.

"You'll do no such thing," the judge shot back. "We're wasting our time here. Unless you have any other futile and pointless statements to make, Counselor, I'll assume this cross-examination is complete."

Mitch looked at his client on the stand. From her expression he knew exactly what she wanted: for him to keep pressing the point, to let her speak and declare the truth in words that could not be denied. But he also know that for the moment, he had pushed the bounds of tolerance in the courtroom as far as he could. He shook his head slightly, trying to convey to her the simple fact that it was better to back off now and hope for another chance later. They may have won the battle, but they were still in terrible danger of losing the war.

"No further questions, Your Honor," he said.

"Then the witness may step down," responded the judge with a sigh of relief.

Helen rose, glaring at the attorney as she returned to the defense table. "Why did you stop?" she demanded in a hoarse whisper as he sat down by her side. "You promised to let me speak."

"You did speak," Mitch whispered, "and you'll speak again. We have to be very careful. This case has to be built one brick at a time."

An angry Helen started to respond, but Mitch cut her off. "Look," he demanded. "I'm your lawyer. Either you trust me or you don't." He glared at her. "What's it going to be?"

"Do I have a choice?" Helen asked ruefully, but she couldn't help but smile as Mitch winked at her.

Chapter 12

AFTER A FIFTEEN-MINUTE RECESS, during which Victoria and Judge Wells disappeared together into his plush office, court was called back into session. Mitch, who'd been excluded from the conference, could only guess at what his rivals were cooking up between them. He didn't have to wait long to find out.

"Does the prosecution have any other witnesses it wishes to call?" the judge asked after he had gaveled the court back into session.

"Just two more, Your Honor," Victoria replied as she gave Mitch an enigmatic look from across the aisle that separated them.

"Proceed," instructed the judge.

Victoria paused dramatically until the courtroom was silent. "The prosecution calls to the stand," she said at last, "Jesus Christ!"

Around them, the spectators erupted into surprised and expectant cries as Victoria's triumphant look to Mitch signaled a new and decidedly unorthodox escalation in the proceedings.

"Objection!" Mitch shouted, jumping to his feet even before he knew what he would say.

"On what grounds, Counselor?" the judge inquired with a malevolent smirk.

"The prosecution is engaging in blatant grandstanding," Mitch replied, thinking on his feet. "She knows perfectly well that the witness she has called has been dead for more than two thousand years."

"Not according to the defendant," Victoria crowed vindictively. "According to Ms. Hannah, this Jesus Christ is alive and well and guiding the lives of His faithful followers even today from His throne in heaven."

Mitch opened his mouth to reply, but nothing came out. He couldn't very well refute Victoria's contention without calling his client a liar. He had walked right into a trap. He turned to look at Helen. The trust he'd asked for was beginning to evaporate. "Objection withdrawn," he said meekly.

Victoria, with a predator's instinct, moved in for the kill. "Of course the objection is withdrawn," she asserted. "Jesus Christ can't come to this stand any more than I can fly to the top of this great building. He's an impotent figment of Helen Hannah's imagination! A powerless creation of her own neediness. And if Jesus Christ did exist, He'd be far too self-absorbed to care about the fate of human beings here on earth. After all, isn't the real criminal on trial here today this so-called Savior? Yet where is He when His followers need Him? Where is this almighty Son of God who demands complete and unquestioning obedience? Jesus!" she shouted the name until it rang from the rafters. "Jesus! Come out, come out wherever You are!"

Like raucous kids at a carnival, the crowd hooted and hollered their derision along with Victoria. She looked up into the gallery and then straight into the camera, making no effort to disguise the wicked gleam in her eyes.

"Mitch!" Helen hissed from her seat beside him. "Stop her! Object! Do something. For her sake—she's mocking God."

Mitch just turned and looked at her, his face impassive. He had already been lured into a legal ambush. He wasn't about to let it happen again.

Victoria, meanwhile, was milking her moment in the spotlight for all it was worth. "This is your chance, Son of God!" she bellowed. "Appear before Your accusers and defend Yourself!" She threw her arms wide. "Come show us poor humans the power and glory that You claim belongs to You alone! Show Yourself now unless, of course, You're a coward. Show Yourself or we'll make You vanish like a bad dream in the morning sunlight!"

During her tirade, the courtroom grew quieter and quieter until an eerie stillness reigned. Victoria stood in the midst of the room, her arms thrown open, her head lifted, and her eyes looking up at the roof, as if daring a bold of lightning to fall from the sky and strike her dead. The faces in the gallery around her reflected a strange new emotion— a palpable fear that perhaps, just maybe, God Himself would answer her summons and appear with the sound of trumpets and a host of angels.

A long moment passed as the silence grew thicker. At last Victoria spoke, and when she did, it was so sudden and loud that the rows of startled people gave out a collective gasp. "That's just what I thought," she sneered. "God and His Son are not only cowards, they are frauds. Plain and simple charlatans whose so-called miracles are nothing more than sleight-of-hand parlor tricks. God isn't real." She pointed a lacquered fingernail at Helen. "He's nothing more than a figment of this woman's imagination. A figment she is willing to kill for!"

The accusation hung in the air like a terrible curse and Helen seemed to crumple under the weight of it. Victoria waited another long minute, while the courtroom spectators held their collective breath. When she spoke again, it was barely above a whisper, one calibrated for maximum dramatic effect. "But I'll tell you a secret," she said, looking straight into the camera's unblinking eye. "The real god is alive and he's here in this courtroom, with us right now. He's here because he wants you to know he is real. He's here because he want you to hear the truth, from his own lips." She turned to the bench. "Your Honor, I call to the stand Franco Macalousso!"

This time the crowd erupted into a deafening roar, like spectators at a playoff game whose team had just scored the tie-breaking run. Judge Wells pounded his gavel in vain as he tried to restore order. The tumult grew even louder as the courtroom doors opened and Franco Macalousso, dressed in a sleek, tailored suit, his hair slicked back off his bony forehead, strode into the room and down the aisle, exuding utter and unassailable confidence.

Marching to the witness stand, the messiah raised his hand to take the oath as the bailiff approached timidly, holding up the ONE Constitution scroll. The crowd's shouts were suddenly silenced as the court official began to speak. "Do you swear," he said, his voice quaking, "to tell the truth, the whole truth, and nothing but the truth for the unity of the people of One Nation Earth?" The scroll trembled in his hand.

"Of course," Macalousso replied, his voice so clear and authoritative it could be heard clearly to the very back rows, and through the forest of microphones dangling in front of him, around the globe. Sitting down, he smiled benevolently as Victoria approached.

"Mr. Macalousso," she began with a mixture of warmth and respect, "do you exist?"

Macalousso's smile became tolerant. "Touch my hands," he invited her. "Feel my flesh. Do I look real to you?"

Victoria nodded and turned back to the cameras, addressing her next question to her worldwide audience. "And why have you come here now? Why have you arrived among us, in flesh and blood, at this exact point in human history?"

Macalousso's answer sounded as if it were addressed to a small and wondering child. He was infinitely patient and infinitely kind as he said, "To save the human race from destruction."

Victoria turned back to him. The tone of her questioning grew sharper. "Save us with miracles and healings?" she asked. "Is that how you will bring salvation?"

Now it was Macalousso's turn to look straight into the cameras. "For two thousand years, the good, simple, and suffering inhabitants of this planet have cried out to the heavens for deliverance." He shook his head sadly. "Have their prayers ever been answered? No!" At the last word his voice became sharply louder, as if accusing God Himself of cruelty and neglect. "All of their worship and adoration have been for nothing! And why?" He leaned forward until his face filled the television screens. "Because they were taught to believe that the power to save them came from beyond." He gestured grandly. "Out there, in heaven. Beyond the sky in some invisible realm."

He rose from his seat and like a loving patriarch addressed his loyal and devoted family. "It's not there," he continued, lifting his finger and pointing upward. "It's never been there." His finger curled into a fist and he struck himself on the chest, right above his heart. The thud echoed in the deathly silent courtroom. "It's in here, my children," he declared with triumph. "That's where the power of transformation has always been and always will be. In our own hearts and minds. Only human beings have the power to save themselves. That's the message I bring to all mankind at this crossroads of history!"

Helen felt pure horror. Could it be that only she could see the deception that lurked behind the grand images and limitless vistas that Macalousso painted with his words? She turned to look at Mitch, but even her lawyer seemed to have fallen under the sway of this spellbinding leader.

"And how," Victoria asked, "do you intend to guide us down the right path of this historic crossroads?"

Macalousso returned to his seat. "That is the simplest, most beautiful part of all," he purred. "Peace and unity will be the signposts the human race will follow. There will be no confusion, no doubt. My promise to all mankind is not of a new heaven coming down to a new earth on some glorious, faraway day. My promise s to make the very earth a heaven . . . here and now!"

Again the gallery erupted into thunderous shouts and applause, only this time Judge Wells joined them, rising up in his robes and clapping his hands enthusiastically.

Victoria, her face alight with admiration, held out her hands as if presenting Macalousso to the waiting world. "A god for today!" she announced loudly, her voice rising above the clamor. "A god for the future! A god for the people! A god for this world!"

The adulation and worship continued unabated as Mitch turned with a pallid and fearful expression to his client. Courtroom tactics were all good and well, his eyes seemed to be saying. But what were all the legal niceties in the book compared to the overwhelming personal magnetism of this majestic individual? He turned, looking across the aisle at Victoria, who had returned to her seat to give Macalousso center stage in the theater that the courtroom had become.

She smiled at him, mixing wicked glee with cruel satisfaction. There could be no question now of who was winning the case and, along with it, the hearts and minds of a watching world.

At last, sated with the unabated worship that poured over him, Macalousso raised his hand for silence. Immediately the deafening noise subsided and the man in the witness stand turned to the judge, handing back the control of the courtroom.

"Does the defense wish to cross-examine?" Judge Wells asked smugly.

Every eye and all cameras turned to Mitch, but it was the gaze of Franco Macalousso that seemed to burn a hole in the attorney's very soul, making him weak in the knees and putting butterflies in his stomach.

Alarmed at his pale and trembling features, Helen reached under the desk to give his hand a reassuring squeeze, only to have him angrily pull away and stand unsteadily to his feet.

"No, Your Honor," Mitch answered. "No questions."

∽

J. T. and Sherri sat side by side on a sprung sofa, watching the live coverage of the trial with expressions of utter amazement. Around them were the others of their small band of outcasts, including the recent additions of Dave and Dawn. Silence filled the cavernous hideout as the resisters watched Helen being taken from the courtroom as the crowd continued to stomp and shout their approval for Franco Macalousso.

As J. T. reached over to turn down the sound, Dawn stood up suddenly, joined quickly by Dave. "Sorry, guys," she said, shaking her head. "But I think this is where we bow out. This rescue of yours is looking more dicey by the minute."

"You got that right," agreed Dave, gathering up his backpack and the suitcase full of guns. "I can tell you right now what my verdict would be if I was one of those judges up there. And it wouldn't be 'Innocent.'"

"Don't be stupid," J. T. replied angrily as he also rose to his feet and confronted them. "Can't you see that this is just a setup? They're manipulating the whole thing. They can make you think whatever they want! Helen is helpless up there. She needs us."

"If they're trying to get us on their side," Dawn countered, "I can tell you right now, it's working. That woman is guilty as sin. Look," she continued, addressing the upturned faces of the others. "It was great meeting you and all. I mean, thanks for the food and the hospitality. But we're out of here."

"Tell you what," Dave added after a moment. "We'll leave you the decoder. Just to show there are no hard feelings."

They began moving toward the subway station exit. "So what does that mean?" J. T. shouted after them. "You're just going to give up? You're going to take the mark like all the rest of them?"

Dawn stopped and turned back. "I don't know what it means," she admitted. "But I'm sure about one thing. You guys have too much heat on you. This whole thing is going to come down hard around your ears if you don't watch your step."

"Dawn, Dave," Sherri pleaded, crossing to the young couple. "Don't you understand? You're the ones who are risking your lives by leaving here. Together we've at least got a chance."

"Yeah," Dawn interjected dryly, "a chance to die."

"I don't know," Dave said hesitantly. "Maybe they're right, Babe. Maybe we've got a better shot of making it through if we hang together."

"You do what you want," his girlfriend replied. "I'm out of here."

Dave watched as she trudged up the stairs and was about to follow when Selma approached and put her hand on his arm. "Please stay," she pleaded. "At least let us try to explain what's really going on out there."

Dave looked around at the expectant faces in the dim light. A long moment passed as he weighed his options and tried his best to see past his own fear. "This better be good," he finally grumbled.

"It's a whole lot better than the lies you've been told," was Selma's fervent reply.

✃

The courtroom was empty except for the two lawyers, one basking in her performance, the other trying to put the shattered pieces of his case back together. Scooping up the last of her legal papers, Victoria made a point of sauntering casually across the aisle where Mitch still sat, staring glumly into space.

"Don't look so down, Sweetheart," she said, her voice oozing with false sincerity. "We all know you're doing the very best you can."

Heading out the courtroom doors, Victoria left Mitch alone with his thoughts but it wasn't long before his painful reflections drove him from his stupor. As he left the building through the back entrance, he passed by the elevator leading to the floor where the prisoners awaiting trial were kept in their holding cells. It was there that two beefy guards stood waiting for a lift with a dejected Helen held in chains between them.

She threw him an accusatory look as he rounded the corner. "I hope you're happy with your day's work, Counselor," she said bitterly. "You let him just sit there, telling his filthy lies to the world. And you didn't say a word."

"Thanks for the update," Mitch shot back as the elevator

bell rang and the door slid open. "In case you were napping at the time, let me clue you in. There wasn't a thing I could do. We were sandbagged, right from the beginning."

Helen shook her head adamantly. "We don't wrestle against flesh and blood," she said, "but against principalities and powers."

"Yeah?" said Mitch sarcastically. "Well, I have news for you. Those principalities are mopping the floor with us."

Helen reached out to take hold of Mitch's hands. "Keep fighting," she whispered, leaning in close before the guards moved in to pull them apart. The lawyer felt her slip a small piece of folded paper into the palm of his hand. "Send this message,' she said urgently into his ear. "You'll get a time and place. They'll give you what you need."

The guards grabbed her by arms and pulled her away, but not before she managed to whisper, "I'm trusting you, Mitch. Just as you asked me to. Don't betray my friends."

Chapter 13

MITCH SAT ALONE BENEATH A POOL of light from the gooseneck lamp on his office desk. Outside, the most of the busy city slept, and only the occasional sound of car tires on the pavement disturbed the peaceful silence out his window. It was his first opportunity in days, Mitch felt, to think, to reflect on the incredible events of the past week, and most importantly, to weigh in his own mind the words of Helen Hannah that echoed there like warning calls in a deep canyon. Was what she claimed true? Was there really a God in heaven above who not only saw and heard everything His creatures did and said, but was active in their simplest and smallest thoughts and actions? Mitch's head began to ache as he struggled with the seeming paradox. If the God of Helen, and the God of his father, were real, why didn't He reach down from above to deliver His followers from their deaths? His father had believed . . . and paid with his life. The same fate almost certainly awaited Helen Hannah, despite Mitch's best efforts. Where was God, Mitch asked himself bitterly, when someone really needed Him?

He sighed. It was too late, and the day had been too long, for him to try and grapple with such weighty questions now. What was required of him at the moment was to focus on the case against his client, and to try and do what he did best—be a good lawyer.

He picked up a file that lay in the desk in front of him, its tab reading "Hannah, Helen," and began flipping through its pages. Photos reflected a younger, more confident and assured woman, at the height of her career as a professional television journalist. Then, as if the photos were part of a time-lapse history of her life, Helen appeared bedraggled and frightened in a police mug shot, staring into the camera with a mix of defiance and defeat. The change could not have been more startling—a trim, well-groomed TV anchorwoman, transformed into a hunted, haunted fugitive. Once again, Mitch couldn't help but think: where was the God to whom Helen Hannah prayed?

He picked up the ONE Security Forces report and scanned the single-spaced lines of type. "Unbreakable." "Defiant." "Unknown reserves of strength." "Impossible to crack." These words and others jumped out at him, while at the same time a black-and-white surveillance camera photo slipped out of the file: in it, Helen, a warm smile on her face, was bending over to offer a homeless person a sandwich and the touch of a caring human being.

Lost in even deeper thought, Mitch searched his shirt pocket until he found the small piece of folded paper Helen had pressed into his hand earlier that day. Opening it up he read the words: "Knock and the door shall open." Turning to the glowing screen of his computer, he quickly typed in the message and, taking a deep breath, hit "Send."

As he waited for the computer to search cyberspace at the speed of light, he opened a drawer in his desk and, reaching far behind a stack of case files, pulled out an old, dog-eared Bible. Opening it to the dedication page, he whispered the words that had been written there in a familiar hand: "To Mitch, my beloved son. May God's face always shine upon you. Love, Dad." Closing the book, Mitch bowed his head and rubbed his eyes. Was he just physically tired, or were the tears that welled up from some deep emotion?

He looked again at the computer screen. A message light blinked and he saw that an e-mail attachment had come over the internet. He was about to hit the command to open the attachment when for the first time he noticed a yellow sticky note at the edge of the pool of light on his desk. He reached over and read the word "Play," with an arrow pointing to where he kept the hidden recorder on his desk. A cold chill raced up his spine as he reached over and hit the play-back button. Who had been in his office? And why?

A voice, soft but sinister, could be heard from the tape speaker, the speaker obviously leaning very closer to the microphone as if conveying an intimate message. "No surprises, Counselor," was the throaty warning. "No surprises."

Mitch shivered, as much from the sudden conviction that he was being watched as from the words on the tape.

He rose stealthily from his desk and making his way to the window, he cracked the blinds and look down on the street below. There, standing in the shadows next to his car, a man dressed in black was barely visible. As Mitch watched, the figure reached into his coat pocket and pulled out a cell phone. A moment later the telephone on his desk jangled and Mitch, startled, jumped back from the window. He let the ring continue for several seconds before picking up the receiver and listening without saying a word.

"Better get some sleep, Counselor," the same voice said. "You're going to need to be in top form tomorrow."

With a click the connection was broken and a moment later Mitch heard the sound of a car motor accelerating down the block and into the night.

He waited for a moment until his heavy heartbeat slowed, thinking to himself how Helen had spoken of the havoc that the Nazis had brought with them. Was this the kind of terror they used to keep their opponents in line? What was next? Murder? Extermination?

He turned back to the light of his computer and with a few keystrokes called the e-mail attachment up onto the screen. It read: "Corner of Capital and Hill, 2 A.M. Come alone."

Mitch glanced at his watch. He'd have to hurry if he was going to get there on time. He crossed to the office door and, taking his jacket off the hanger, was about to leave when he noticed a late edition of the day's paper lying on a chair. The front-page photo showed Franco Macalousso as he had testified on the stand that afternoon. The look in his eyes seemed to promise so much—peace and prosperity and a better world for all mankind. But for the first time, Mitch thought he could detect another message being conveyed by those magnetic eyes, a message of warning, a command to obey or else. The uncanny picture seemed to be staring directly at him, and as he slipped his hand into his jacket pocket to search for his car keys, he found instead a small card distributed widely around town at every newsstand and market counter. On it was a phone number to call, any time of day or night, to report Hater activity or to turn in a suspected enemy of the new government. Mitch looked at the card for a long moment, his thoughts in turmoil, then slipped it back into his pocket and walked through the door, heading into the night.

∽

Ninety minutes later, Mitch found himself in a situation that would have evoked scornful laughter if it had been suggested to him even twenty-four hours earlier. With a hardly a moment to reflect on how he had gotten there, Mitch was being led down an abandoned subway tunnel by two strange men in dirty clothes who appeared to be brothers. All around them the dripping of water and the scurrying of rats set up a nerve-wracking accompaniment, but Mitch's guides seemed unruffled by their damp and dim journey. They were experienced in staying invisible, keeping under the radar of the ONE police, and Mitch knew instinctively that this was no game—these Haters were playing for keeps.

The subway tunnel terminated in an abandoned station where a camp of some sort had been set up, complete with computer terminals, cots for sleeping, and a primitive kitchen with propane camp stoves and picnic coolers to keep the supplies from spoiling. His guides, who had introduced themselves as Jake and Tony, pointed to the flickering light of an oil-drum fire at one end of the station where a group of ragged and dirt-smudged people were huddled. A black woman with a bright smile broke away from the others as he approached.

"Mr. Kendrick," she said, reaching out to touch him on the shoulder. "Thanks for getting in touch with us. My name is Selma Davis, and I've been praying specifically for God to bring you alongside to help us in our struggle."

A young man with an angry look on his face joined them and, cutting off Selma's greeting, demanded, "Why didn't you use that tape?"

Mitch swallowed his impulse to turn and run. This was most definitely more than he'd bargained for. He'd landed smack in the middle of a Haters' lair and they seemed to know a lot more about him then he did about them.

"I'm here, aren't I?" he snapped back at his accuser.

"Give him a break, J. T.," Selma urged her comrade.

"Why should I?" J. T. replied, his eyes narrowing suspiciously.

"Because I believe you're innocent in the death of those

schoolchildren," Mitch promptly responded. "That tape proved as much. But I am going to need a lot more than the word of one man on a fuzzy videotape to make a case in court."

"So we should trust you," J. T. snarled, "just like that?"

Mitch shrugged. "Like it or not, I'm the only chance Helen's got."

J. T. raised his eyebrows and said to Selma out of the side of his mouth, "I guess we better start praying harder."

"Hey," Mitch replied just as sarcastically, "What do you want me to do? Start singing a rousing chorus of 'Amazing Grace' when court opens tomorrow?"

The two faced off. "You keep that up," J. T. threatened, "and you're going to need a lot more than amazing grace."

Sherri, who had moved up behind her husband during this heated verbal exchange, promptly stepped between the two of them. "That's quite enough of that, boys," she cautioned, then turned to Mitch. "I don't mean to pry," she continued, "but maybe you could tell us why, exactly, you've suddenly shown up here."

Mitch stepped back and looked at each of the rebels in turn. "Look," he said at last. "I'm doing the best I can up there. But no matter what I do, and no matter what Helen might say in her own defense, no one's going to accept her story unless I can back it up. You're her friends. Maybe you should think of coming forward instead of cowering down here, waiting for a miracle."

Now it was the outlaws' turns to exchange looks, as each

waited for the other to make the first move. It was Selma who finally took a step forward. "If you need me," she said, swallowing hard, "I'll be there. Just tell me when and where."

Jake, with an alarmed look, grabbed her arm. "What are you talking about, Selma?"

"I'm going to testify, just as the lawyer said," Selma replied firmly. "I'm going to take the stand for Helen. I know she'd do the same for me."

"You understand what this means," continued Mitch. "Appearing in court as a Hater means you'll be turning yourself in to the ONE forces."

"You mean leave this five-star resort?" Selma replied, looking around the dank subway station with a laugh. But a moment later, the laughter faded and she faced the others with a look of grim determination. "Helen is my friend," she asserted. "She's one of us. And if she needs me now, how can I turn away and pretend not to hear?" She paused, searching for the right words. "It's more than just standing up for Helen," she continued at last. "It's standing up for faith . . . for what I believe." She turned and looked directly at J. T. "I know how you feel, sitting down here and doing nothing when one of our own is being crucified," she said. "Well, believe it or not, I feel the same way. Maybe this is my chance to do something."

J. T. shook his head angrily and glared at Mitch. "There's a difference between being courageous and going to the slaughter like a lamb."

His words put a chill into the already cold air of the station. For a long moment nobody spoke. At last Mitch cleared his throat and stepped forward. "Look," he began, "I can't pretend to understand what makes you people tick. But I do know this. I couldn't live with your deaths on my conscience. Whether or not any of you wants to sacrifice your life by appearing in court is up to you. What I need is hard evidence." He thought for a moment. "Like that detonator the ONE Agent Sweig was holding in the video. That might help the cause."

"No problem there," piped in Tony. "We've got that and a bunch of other things that could be useful too." He turned to his brother. "Let's round up the evidence," he said.

"We can have it for you in a couple of hours," enthused Jake.

"Great!" Mitch replied. "I can use anything and everything that might help the cause."

Selma stepped forward and fixed the lawyer with an intense gaze. "I mean it," she said to him. "Whenever you want me to step forward and tell the truth, I'll be there. You know how to reach us now. Don't ever think I wouldn't do what's right for my sister."

"I know you would," Mitch reassured her. "But I don't think it's going to be necessary. You may be willing to risk your life for this faith of yours, but I couldn't be the one to send you out to the wolves." He put his hand on her arm. "We'll find another way, Selma." With that, he turned and in a few moments had disappeared into the gloom of the subway tunnel, returning the way he had come and leaving the outlaws alone in their hideout.

J. T. snorted with disgust as he watched Mitch vanish in the shadows. "That fool is going to get Helen killed," he grumbled. "There's just no way anything good could ever come out of this."

Tony nodded in agreement. "I'm with J. T.," he vowed. "It's one thing for Helen to die for what she believes. But it's something else when all she's doing is giving the world — like bloodthirsty Romans in the coliseum — what it wants. I don't want any part of that."

Sherri took her husband's hand and looked deep into his eyes. "I had my doubts," she said, "all this violence, taking God's law into our own hands." She smiled affectionately. "But maybe you're right after all, J. T. Maybe the only way to save Helen is to take direct action. Let's hear your plan." Her eyes flashed a warning. "But remember," she added, "Helen wouldn't want any of us to die for her . . . or to kill for her."

J. T. turned to look down the now-empty tunnel. "I don't trust that lawyer," he said ominously. "I don't think he knows what side he's on."

Sherri reached up and, holding J. T.'s chin, and turned her husband's face back toward her. "Hey," she reminded him gently, "he's not the only one with a false mark on him." She smiled. "If we can't trust him, maybe we can't trust you, either." The couple shared a chuckle and a swift, strong hug.

It was in that moment that the world in which they had found refuge, hidden from the forces of vengeance unleashed by Macalousso and his ONE security squad, came crashing down around them in a sudden and horrific explosion of violence. Even as J. T. and Sherri shared the warmth of each other's arms, a loud buzzer and a flashing red light came to life at the far end of the tunnel. There was no doubt in any of the rebels' minds exactly what the warning meant. Their perimeter had been breached. The enemy was at the door.

Jake turned to Dave, who stood paralyzed with fear near the oil-can fire. "Quick!" he commanded, grabbing him by the arm. "Follow me! This way!"

They joined the others who had already scurried to the back of the subway station where, working frantically, they began to push aside a large piece of rusted metal support, revealing the gaping hole of a ventilation shaft on the far side. Climbing into it one by one, they slid down its slick sides and into the utter dark of the cylinder. The last one in was Tony, who turned back to see Sherri and J. T. still at the computer terminals, desperately gathering as many files and disks as they could to keep the secrets of the resistance safe from Macalousso's thugs.

"Come on!" he shouted, but it was already too late. A tremendous explosion rocked the station, throwing Tony down the shaft and filling the subway confines with dust and debris. In the chaos, J. T. was hurled backward by the impact, the gun he had in his hands ripped away and sent skittering across the floor and down onto the tracks. "Sherri!" he shouted through the smoke and dust, but there was no answer, his wife lost in the swirling confusion.

All around him, beams of light probed the thick air and, a moment later, ONE agents with flashlights mounted on their guns emerged into the station platform. The atmosphere had cleared enough for J. T. to see his wife lying prone on the floor a short distance away, with a ONE agent standing over her with a gun pointed at her head. Slowly Sherri raised her hands in surrender as J. T. began looking frantically around for another weapon. Then, a few feet away, he saw a semiautomatic pistol thrown by the force of the explosion to the floor. He tensed himself, getting ready to spring for it.

He stopped when the agent standing over Sherri turned and looked directly at him, an evil smile spreading across his face. Without moving the gun away from her temple, his words echoed in J. T.'s brain like a sentence of death pronounced by a black-hooded executioner. "What ever happened to turning the other cheek, Hater?" the agent sneered.

As if in agonizing slow motion, J. T. watched helplessly as the next deadly sequence of events unfolded. Realizing now that he would never reach the gun in time, J. T. looked at his wife, who returned his gaze with an expression that seemed to sum up all the love they shared, even as it wordlessly conveyed how much she would miss him now. A feeling of utter helplessness welled up in J. T.'s heart as he realized there was nothing he could do to save his wife's life.

The agent, meanwhile, was looking back down at his victim, the malicious smile now frozen on his lips. Deliberately and without a tremor of hesitation he sent two shots crashing through her brain and watched dispassionately as the young woman's lifeless eyes fixed on her husband.

"No!" screamed J. T. with the deafening echo of the gunshots still ringing in his ears. "No!" He dove for the pistol even as another of the agents opened fire on him, peppering the ground at his feet with bullets. In the next moment more firing was heard, and through a haze of rage and despair J. T. could see Tony crawling out of the ventilation duct, guns blazing in each hand. The agents ran for cover as J. T. finally laid hold of the gun and began firing at them, letting all his emotions flow through his trigger finger and into the hail of hot metal.

Joining Tony near the escape route, J. T. continued firing with wild abandon at anything that moved. Suddenly, next to him, Tony groaned and dropped to the ground, clutching his chest. J. T. knelt long enough to pry one of the weapons from the dead man's fingers before continuing to return fire at the approaching agents.

The one that had killed his wife suddenly moved to the forefront, pulling a hand grenade from a loop on his belt. Yanking out the pin with his teeth, he sent it flying in J. T.'s direction and again the subway station was rocked by a deafening explosion.

When the smoke cleared, fallen beams and large chunks of concrete blocked the ventilation duct. The agents searched frantically but the body of their quarry, the Hater known only as J. T., was nowhere to be found.

Chapter 14

THE COURTROOM HAD BECOME a familiar sight to the worldwide audience who tuned in every day to watch the latest installment of the trial of the millennium. It had brought work of every description to a virtual standstill during the dramatic sessions. Today, the third in *ONE v Helen Hannah*, was no exception and the excited buzz that filled the chambers was as loud and persistent as it had been on the very first day of the trial.

The prosecution and defense had taken their places behind tables on either side of the central aisle, but their contrasting moods could hardly have been more different. Victoria Thorne was still basking in the glow of her brilliant coup of yesterday when Franco Macalousso himself took the stand to demonstrate clearly his clear superiority to the superstition and ignorance of the defendant. For his part, Mitch Kendrick could only glance anxiously at his watch and crane his neck to the back of the room, as if waiting for a late arrival.

"I don't know what happened to your so-called friends,"

he said irritably to his client. "But if I had to guess I'd say they had second thoughts about helping you out of this jam."

Helen shook her head. "I don't believe that for a minute," she countered. "Something must have happened. If they said they were going to be here, then they will be. And they'll bring the evidence with them. I'm sure of it." She turned to smile reassuringly at Mitch, only then noticing that his attention had been distracted by the prosecution.

Victoria was staring across at both of them with a subtle smile flickering at the corners of her mouth. As Helen watched with a puzzled expression, the attorney held up her wrist and pointed deliberately at the watchband.

It took Mitch only a moment to catch on to the message being telegraphed by Victoria. With a sudden motion he tore his own watch off his wrist and, turning it over, discovered the small homing device Victoria had planted there two days earlier.

With a shocked expression, he held it up for Helen to see. "I . . . I . . . " he stammered, "I . . . don't know how this happened. Somehow she got a tracking chip on me." He looked over to Victoria, whose wicked smile had widened.

Helen was staring at the prosecutor too, a look of pure contempt on her face.

"I'm sorry," Mitch mumbled. "If I'd only known . . . "

Helen turned her gaze to him, her eyes now filled with tears.

Mitch flinched at the disappointment and sorrow he saw there. So preoccupied was he by the treacherous discovery that Mitch failed to notice the arrival of Judge Wells, who immediately brought the court to order and ordered the defense to call its first witness of the day.

"Is there a problem, Mr. Kendrick?" the judge asked impatiently when Mitch failed to respond.

"No, Your Honor," Mitch replied, snapping out of his stupor and standing to his feet, trying desperately to collect his thoughts. "I would like to request a recess," he said finally.

"Denied," the judge snapped back. "Call a witness or rest your case."

"But—" Mitch began, with a sinking sensation in the pit of his stomach.

At that moment, a loud alarm could be heard blaring from the back of the courtroom and Mitch turned with the rest of the gallery to witness a small, raggedly dressed black woman being detained at the mark detector by several ONE guards.

"Selma!" shouted Helen, simultaneously delighted to see her old friend and horrified by the manhandling she was receiving at the hands of the guards.

Mitch, with sudden inspiration, turned to face Judge Wells. "Your Honor," he said confidently, "I'd like to call Selma Davis to the stand."

The judge shot a glare at him but could not contest the request and, with a petulant signal to the guards, had Selma released and brought to the stand.

As she passed the defense table, she stopped, reaching

down to embrace her friend. "Be of good courage, sister," she whispered. "He is with us."

"What happened?' Mitch demanded in a low tone. "Where's the evidence you promised?"

Selma looked up at him with haunted eyes. "I don't know how," she reported, "but they found us. We barely escaped and . . . " she turned to face Helen "Sherri and J. T. didn't make it."

Helen choked back a sob, looking over to Mitch with an accusatory expression. They both knew how the ONE agents had found the hideout.

Mitch cleared his throat and turned to Selma. "You don't have to do this, you know," he reminded her.

She just smiled. "If you believed," she replied, "then you'd understand."

"Mr. Kendrick," the judge snarled, "the court is waiting, if you don't mind."

Selma made her way forward to the witness stand and Mitch had just enough time to give Victoria a sardonic smile before he followed Selma to the front of the courtroom to begin his questioning.

He whispered as he leaned over the railing of the witness stand, "Don't be too . . . " Then he paused, searching for the word.

"Christian?" Selma whispered back with a smile.

Mitch shrugged ruefully. "I was going to say 'radical,'" he admitted. "But I guess you get the idea."

The bailiff approached, holding the by-now-familiar

scroll. Selma just shook her head. "You're going to get the same answer from me that you got from Helen," she warned him and gestured at the scroll. "I wouldn't touch that thing with a ten-foot pole." She turned to Judge Wells and said, "But I do swear to tell the truth."

Judge Wells glared at her. "Proceed, Counselor," he told Mitch.

"Ms. Davis," the lawyer began, "you are a member of the underground group known as the Haters. Is this not true?"

Selma wrinkled her nose. "I never did care for that name," she replied. "But I am proud to be counted as a born-again child of God."

Mitch pointed to where Helen sat at the defense table. "And the defendant," he continued, "is she also a member of this group?"

Selma smiled warmly at Helen. "She is a brave sister in Christ," she replied. "And she is my beloved friend."

Mitch nodded, then began to pace in front of the stand. "You took great personal risks to come and testify here today, did you not, Ms. Davis?"

Selma shrugged. "I could be killed for what I believe, if that what's you mean."

"Objection," interrupted Victoria petulantly. "That is pure conjecture."

"Sustained," said Judge Wells.

The legal wrangling seemed to catch Mitch off guard. Stalling for time to come up with another approach, he returned to the defense table and flipped through his notepad.

"Counselor," the judge queried impatiently, "do you wish to proceed or are we to assume that you have finished with this witness?"

Helen leaned forward and in a hushed and urgent tone, exhorted her lawyer: "She's giving up her life to come here," she reminded him. "Don't let her die in vain. Just search your heart for the right questions."

Mitch looked deeply into her eyes and, after a moment, his face lighted up with sudden inspiration. He turned back to the witness stand just as the judge was about to bark another order at him. "Could you tell us why it is that the God you worship didn't appear on behalf of the defendant yesterday?" he asked.

Selma shook her head. "God does not obey the will of man. He acts or does not act as He pleases."

"But Franco Macalousso," Mitch insisted, "he came. He spoke. He made himself known to the world."

"Of course he did," Selma agreed. "And God was right here among us, watching the whole thing."

"But where was He?" Mitch insisted and for an answer, Selma simply placed her hand directly over her heart.

From the prosecution table Victoria snorted derisively.

"I don't understand," admitted Mitch. "If God is everywhere, including people's hearts, why didn't He make Himself known? Why didn't He defend Himself and save His loyal follower?"

"He could have come down off the cross too," Selma patiently explained. "He could have defended Himself when they were mocking and scourging Him. But what we have so much trouble understanding is that God's ways are not our ways. If you think about the resurrection—"

"Objection!" Victoria shouted. "This resurrection she's talking about is nothing more than an unsubstantiated myth. We might as well be talking about fairy tales here. It's a contention the witness has no way of proving."

"Just try me," Selma shot back and from her chair, it was all Helen could do to keep from cheering.

A silence now reigned in the courtroom. Mitch cast a quick glance at the witness, remembering the words Helen had spoken to him: *Ask the questions that are in your heart.*

"Isn't it true," he continued at last, "that the resurrection you speak of is the central tenet of the Christian faith that you profess?"

Selma nodded.

"And isn't it also true," he continued, "that if such an event never happened, your faith would be based on nothing?"

Selma just looked at him, letting the question hang in the air. A long moment passed.

"Continue," said Judge Wells at last.

"Your Honor," interjected Mitch, turning to face the bench. "If it pleases the court, the defense will ask no further questions of this witness." He nodded slightly toward Victoria. "The prosecution is free to cross-examine her on the reality of the resurrection."

A murmur rose in the courtroom. Not a single one of the billions who watched around the world could fail to see that the gauntlet had been dropped. Victoria would have to accept.

"It pleases the court," Judge Wells announced, and the smile on his face was a clear indication of his belief that Victoria would demolish Selma in short order. "What says the prosecution?"

Victoria shot a look at Mitch, as if to say she was wise to his ploy. She knew he had put her on the spot, but she'd been on the spot before and had always been able to turn it into the spotlight. Today would be no different. "With pleasure, Your Honor," she replied and strode to the front of the courtroom.

"Ms. Davis," she began in an aggressive and arrogant tone, "am I correct in assuming that you wish to have this court believe that two thousand years ago a man named Jesus, who was allegedly the Son of God Himself, was nailed to a cross and died, only to rise from the dead three days later?"

"That's the fact," replied Selma.

Victoria sighed. "This so-called miracle occurred more than twenty centuries ago. Yet you claim to be able to prove that it actually happened?"

"Yes."

Victoria made a show of stifling a giggle. "Excuse me for laughing, Ms. Davis," she said, "but since we have trouble establishing events that happened last week, how do you propose to prove the life, death, and resurrection of this Jesus?"

Selma looked past Victoria to the press gallery with its crowd of TV cameramen. "Jesus of Nazareth is as established a figure as any other individual in human history. If you decided that there was not enough evidence to prove His existence, then you'd have to question the existence of Caesar and Aristotle and a thousand other well-known figures from the past."

Victoria hesitated for a beat, betraying the slightest stirrings of self-doubt, but shook them off as soon as they appeared. "I didn't ask you if Jesus was a real person," she insisted. "What I asked you for was proof that He died and returned from the grave."

Selma crossed her arms and cocked her eyebrow. "Let me ask you a question," she parried. "How many witnesses does it take to win a conviction, Ms. Thorne?"

Victoria frowned. She didn't know where this was going but she didn't like the sound of it. "One," she replied brusquely.

"Well, then," Selma continued relentlessly, "what would you say about an event that was attested to by more than five hundred witnesses? There are no less than five hundred documented accounts of folks who saw our Lord and Savior after He was raised from the dead."

"People also claim to have seen little green men from Mars," the prosecutor scoffed. Laughter greeted her rebuff, but Selma was unfazed. "We're talking about five hundred respected individuals," she insisted. "These were people who could easily be challenged, even persecuted, for what they said. But in the face of adversity, they stuck to their stories."

"Respected?" Victoria spat the word back. "Please, Ms. Davis. Isn't it a fact that some of these 'respected' witnesses you speak of were tax gatherers and fishermen—no better than common rabble? I would hardly characterize them as pillars of society."

Selma nodded. "Sure enough," she admitted. "Some of them were men who ran away the moment Jesus was arrested, a bunch of men who denied His name when they honestly believed He was the Messiah sent by God. But it was this same group of cowards who, three days after the crucifixion, rose up with a new power and conviction and a total commitment to the Christ they had betrayed with their actions. They were the same men who preached His gospel throughout the whole world."

Victoria cast a meaningful look at Mitch. "Some men will do anything to become famous," she sneered.

"They were mocked and tortured and killed for what they preached," Selma countered. "That's hardly lusting after fame. If Christ had died and stayed in the grave, these men long since would have been forgotten in the march of time."

"Objection, Your Honor," said a suddenly flustered Victoria.

"You can't object to your own cross-examination," Judge Wells reminded her sternly.

The prosecutor took a deep breath. She needed to pull herself together. What had looked like an easy mop-up operation was turning out to be a major embarrassment. She needed a new strategy and she needed it quickly.

Turning to face the courtroom and the cameras, Victoria tried a new tactic. "We've heard the witness talk about a lot of ancient history, here, ladies and gentlemen. Ancient history out of musty old books. That's where the Haters have always put their faith, in fairy tales from a long-forgotten past. But what about modern times? What about contemporary evidence that stands up to contemporary standards? That seems to be sorely missing from Ms. Davis's testimony."

Selma listened impassively. "Do you know who Simon Greenleaf is?" she asked.

The question took Victoria back, but only for a moment. "Of course I do," she replied imperiously. "He was the founder of the Harvard School of Law. Mr. Greenleaf was considered the world's greatest authority on legal standards of evidence."

"That's right, Ms. Thorne," said Selma as if she were awarding a gold star to a prize pupil. "Well, that same Mr. Greenleaf was once presented with the account of Jesus' death and resurrection. He pored over all the testimonies, thoroughly reviewed the facts, discarded everything that might be considered inadmissible in a court of law, and concluded that, based strictly on the evidence, the resurrection is as established a fact as any other well-documented event in the history of mankind. He even—"

"Objection!" Victoria shrilly interrupted. "No . . . no more questions," she stammered.

"Finally," a clearly distressed Judge Wells whispered under his breath. He banged the gavel with a vengeance. "Court is adjourned."

Turning to a phalanx of ONE security agents who stood nearby, he pointed to Selma, who sat without flinching in the witness stand. "Guards," he commanded, "arrest this woman as an enemy of One Nation Earth."

He turned to the defense and prosecution lawyers. "Counselors," he continued in a low and ominous voice, "in my chambers, immediately."

There was no mistaking what was beneath his words. Both Mitch and Victoria had a lot of explaining to do.

Chapter 15

JUDGE WELLS BURST INTO HIS CHAMBERS, his black robes flying and his face red with anger at the events that had unfolded in his courtroom. It wasn't simply that a trial that was supposed to be his finest judicial hour seemed to be slipping, moment by moment, further from his control. There were other, even more important stakes in this deadly serious contest. The august judge knew perfectly well that if the expected outcome was not achieved, he himself would be answerable to none other than Franco Macalousso and he had seen enough of the messiah's brand of justice to shudder at such a prospect. Someone was going to have to answer for the fiasco that Helen Hannah's trial was becoming . . . and he knew exactly who that would be.

Waiting for him nervously in the plush leather chairs of his office were Victoria and Mitch, both sharing the same nervous look. When Judge Wells stormed in, they both jumped, their heads swiveling around to watch him approach.

"I'd be looking over my shoulder too," he stormed at

them, "if I were in your shoes. What's the meaning of that outrage in my courtroom today?" He glared at them, his arms crossed. "Well?" he huffed. "I'm waiting for an explanation. And it better be good."

"Don't look at me," Victoria whined. "It's Kendrick who's causing all the trouble." She turned to the defense lawyer with a withering look. "You're not even trying to follow the script!"

Mitch shrugged and tried to stifle a smile. "I'm not the one who blew the cross-examination of Selma Davis," he replied.

Victoria's face grew pale with rage. "No," she hissed, "but you were the one who called her to the stand in the first place. That wasn't exactly part of the plan."

"How was I to know she was going to turn up all of a sudden?" he asked innocently, then couldn't help but add, "Maybe you should have done a little more homework on the Simon Greenleaf issue."

Sputtering with sheer outrage, Victoria turned to Judge Wells. "Do you believe this?" she demanded. "He's in with the Haters! I'm sure of it. How else could he have gotten that woman to risk her life by appearing in court today?"

The judge stroked his chin thoughtfully, then turned to Mitch and asked with an ominous edge to his voice, "Care to answer that question, Counselor?"

"My instructions were clear," Mitch replied promptly. "I was told to win their confidence. And that's exactly what I did. Sure, I went to their hideout." He turned to Victoria, his eyes narrowing. "But I guess you already knew that, didn't you, Madame Prosecutor?"

"Well," the judge ventured, "I can't say whether you were just doing your job or if you have taken on the unfortunate tendency of other defense lawyers I have known to become sympathetic to their clients. But I do know that if you were in contact with a Haters group, it is your responsibility as a citizen of ONE to report its whereabouts as soon as possible. I will not have any further demonstrations of Hater dramatics in my courtroom. Is that understood?"

Mitch and Victoria traded a poisonous look, but even as he showed his defiance, the defense lawyer knew his options were running out. Reluctantly, he pulled the small card with the Hater reporting number on it. Flipping it over, he handed it to the judge.

"What's this?" Wells demanded, staring at a series of number and letters scrawled on the back.

"It's a license-plate number I got last night after I left the Hater hideout," Mitch said in a low tone. He hung his head, trying to avoid the eyes of the others as they fixed on him. "I wasn't able to get any more information and somehow I don't think they're going to trust me enough to get close again. If you're going to round them up, you'll have to run a trace on those plates. It's the best I can do."

"Do you actually think they'd be able to get their hands on a car?" asked Victoria.

"They're more resourceful than we can imagine," Mitch replied. "And what they can't buy, they could certainly steal."

Judge Wells turned the card between his fingers, thinking for a long moment. "If you think this is going to be some sort of 'get out of jail free' card for you, Kendrick," he said at last, "think again. You've already got a lot to answer for. Making this trial look authentic is one thing. But making ONE look bad before the eyes of the whole world is quite another. I don't want any more surprises out there. We end this trial tomorrow as planned. And the verdict is going to be as determined. Nothing less will do. Let's wrap this up with a flourish." He glared at both of them and added, "Because, and let me make myself perfectly clear on this point, if I get called to the chopping block on this, I'm going to make absolutely certain I take you two along with me."

◊◊

In the courthouse surveillance room, the two hapless ONE agents, Shearer and Cantona, were once again puzzling over the sudden interruption of the transmission from the holding cell of Helen Hannah. One moment, the sound and picture had been clear and steady. They had watched as the prisoner's attorney, Mitch Kendrick, had entered the room and in the next second, the screen and the speaker where clogged with static.

"Oh, boy," sighed a frustrated Shearer. "Here we go again." He reached over and picked up the receiver of the console telephone.

"Hold on a second," said his partner with alarm. "Let's

try and fix this thing ourselves. I don't want this going on the report again."

"No way," replied Shearer. "I got strict orders to report any break in this feed. Word goes directly to Ms. Thorne and that's one lady I'd rather not tangle with, if you don't mind."

Cantona shuddered. "I hear you," he said as his partner punched up Victoria's direct line.

❧

Mitch remained silent as he set down the scrambler on the table between him and his client. Helen could see clearly the troubled look on his face and was about to speak when Mitch cut her off with a sudden gesture. "Look," he said, "let's just cut the small talk. Things aren't going well. That's all you need to know."

Helen reached over and touched his hand lightly with her fingers. "I'm sure you won't believe this," she said with sympathy, "but I'm sorry, truly sorry that you're having to go through all of this."

"You sound just like my dad," Mitch responded. "He said the same thing to me." He looked straight into Helen's eyes and his troubled, self-absorbed expression faded. "You know," he continued with a sad smile, "I can't believe that with all that you've got hanging over you, my little problems could concern you in the least. I mean, in a couple of days . . . " He swallowed hard, unable to finish his sentence. He turned away, but after a moment, looked back at her, the look on his face now one of genuine respect. "I guess it's because you actually believe that you'll be going to a better place, is that it?"

Helen smiled as if to relieve Mitch of the burden of his dark conjectures. In the meeting of their eyes, they both found a precious and tender moment of respite from the madness that was swirling everywhere around them. "Mitch," she said, her voice full of sincerity and empathy, "please try to understand. Now, more than ever, I need to get up on that stand to testify. This trial has made me see, all over again, how much God loves me—how much He sacrificed for me . . . for us. I've got to try and get that message across. If I can reach just one person, if I can rescue just one soul from the deception that's all around us, then it will be worth it."

Mitch's eyes began to glisten with tears, but at the same time his face hardened into anger. He was clearly struggling with the conflicting emotions that Helen's words had evoked. "Still so willing to die?" he asked bitterly. "Come on, Helen. Don't be so ready to throw your life away. Don't be like my dad. I begged him to give them what they wanted, but he just wouldn't listen. I don't want to see you make the same mistake."

"Your dad saw the truth for what it was," Helen answered intently. "He knew that two plus two equals four. No matter what anyone else might say."

Mitch leaped to his feet. "What difference does it make now?" he shouted in anger. "Why can't you see that staying alive is more important than any principle, any truth?" He threw up his hands. "I've tried to understand it from your point of view. I even prayed that if there were a God, He would make a move, any move, to help you out of this. But I never got an answer. And I never will."

"That's because you're trying to get God to do what you want Him to do," Helen answered calmly. "Pray instead to know what His will is for you. And for me."

"But I'm trying to save the life of one of His followers!" Mitch shot back, his voice cracking in anguish. "I'm trying to defend Him against a disbelieving world. Isn't this great God of yours supposed to come to the aid of those who call out to Him?"

"He will," Helen replied, her eyes alight with an inner fire. "You've got to have faith, Mitch. He won't let us down. Not if you believe."

"Faith!" Mitch's voice raised a notch. "I need help, Helen, not faith. I need protection and so do you." He threw his arms wide. "Look around you. Wake up. There's no cavalry coming over the hill to rescue us. You're not going to be snatched from the jaws of death in the nick of time. You're about to die for a God who may not even exist. A God who hasn't lifted a finger to help you."

"That's not true, Mitch," replied Helen, pleading with her eyes. "God gave His life for us."

"Spare me," Mitch's shouted. "I've heard it all before from my father! God's 'love' and God's 'mercy'—try coming down from that cloud and living in the real world for once in your life!"

"Your father loved you," Helen said, choking back a sob. "He cared very much about you."

"No!" Mitch was now screaming, the tears flowing down his cheeks. "My father cared about God! He loved God! That's all he ever loved!" He slammed his fist on the table, and in his grief and anger, didn't notice the jamming device falling from its perch. As it hit the floor, the small blinking red light flickered and went out.

Instantly, in the surveillance bunker far below them, the static that had hidden their meeting from prying eyes disappeared and at that same moment, Victoria Thorne burst into the room. The two ONE security agents exchanged a quick look of relief as the prosecutor crossed to the monitor that showed Mitch and Helen in the middle of their angry and intense confrontation.

"I should have gone with my gut and used an insanity plea," Mitch was saying as he paced the perimeter of the small room. "I try to help and all I get from you is platitudes and pious speeches. I'm sick of all this talk about faith and God and believing. This is the real world we're living in! Get real!"

A satisfied smile spread across Victoria's face as she listened. It was obvious that the defendant and her lawyer were not exactly seeing eye to eye, which was going to make it that much easier to bring this case to it foreordained conclusion.

"I tried to help you," Mitch said, his words sharp with bitterness. "I tried to protect you from what they had planned.

Don't you understand how I put myself and my career at risk, even by trying to keep them from overhearing us?"

Victoria's smile disappeared. "He's up to something," she said to the agents. "Get some men down there and search that cell immediately."

"But—" Shearer began, then suddenly stopped when he saw the look in the prosecutor's eye. He grabbed the phone and hurriedly punched up a string of numbers.

Victoria stared again at the video monitor, her eyes narrowing as she listened to Mitch's rant.

"You're just like my dad!" he shouted as Helen flinched at the anger in his voice. "Your eyes are so blinded by that brilliant white light of heaven that you're always talking about that you can't even see what's right in front of you!" He turned to leave just as two beefy guards burst into the cell.

"Hold it right there, Mr. Kendrick," one of them commanded. "We have orders to search you here and now."

"What?" Mitch sputtered. "Whose orders? This is ridiculous! I demand—"

His words were cut short as the guard shoved him against the wall and quickly but thoroughly searched him from head to foot. "He's clean," the guard reported, looking into the mounted camera, then turned to Mitch. "You're free to go."

Moving toward Helen, they didn't notice the prisoner quickly knock the jamming device under the table, trying desperately to hide it. As Mitch hurried out, the guards moved on the defenseless woman, the hands rudely grabbing her body until one of them happened to notice the small box lying under the table. With a leering smile, he reached over and picked it up, holding it triumphantly in front of the video camera in the corner of the room.

✿

In a rundown hotel lobby on a forgotten avenue deep in the heart of the city's darkest and most desperate quarter, a group of derelicts and dispossessed people gathered around a television set, their deeply lined faces lighted by the flickering glow of the tube. In the shadows in one corner of the dusty, threadbare room, a familiar figure lurked as if afraid to expose herself to even the feeble light of the TV. It was Dawn, alone with her condemning thoughts of having deserted the only person she had ever loved, along with a band of people who had tried only to help her. The memories of her encounter with the group of Haters in their subway hideout were still vivid and for the hundredth time since she had run from them, she wondered if it had been the right thing to do. Dave had stayed and cast his lot with the Christians. Maybe she should have done the same. At least she wouldn't be here, hiding from her own shadows in a fleabag hotel lobby.

The image on the TV screen showed the same earnest face of the reporter who had been covering Helen Hannah's trial from the first day. "Court proceedings in what has been called the most important trial in human history took an unexpected turn today," she was saying. "To the surprise of many, Helen Hannah's defense attorney, Mitch Kendrick, called to the stand a known Hater and Christian terrorist, Selma Davis, as a surprise witness for the defense."

At the sound of the name, Dawn's eyes widened. Despite her fear, she began to move closer to the screen.

∞

In a battered and windowless van not far from the hotel where Dawn was intently watching the evening news, three men sat crouched over a mobile TV monitor. Two of them wore official ONE agent uniforms, while the third was dressed for action in dark clothes and a utility belt.

"Here to shed further light on this bizarre turn of events," continued the reporter on the screen, "is our own legal expert, Kathleen Walker."

A trim, no-nonsense woman appeared on the screen, looking straight into the camera. "'Bizarre' is certainly an apt term for today's courtroom dramatics," she remarked. "Kendrick refused to cross-examine a credible witness and chose instead to put this known outlaw on the stand."

The man nearest the television reached over and snapped off the power. "Credible witness," scoffed J. T., adjusting the tight-fitting collar of the ONE uniform wore, stolen from a dry cleaning store in preparation for this very operation. "Who do they think they're kidding?"

"The sooner we get this over with, the better," added Dave Sands, who was also disguised as a ONE agent. He turned to Jake Goss, who had slipped a small screwdriver from his utility belt and was making a minor adjustment to a small black box in his hands. "You know how to operate that thing?" Dave asked.

"I think so," Jake replied. "Looks like your girlfriend made it pretty idiot proof." He smiled grimly before adding, "Not that I'm an idiot or anything." He handed the box to Dave, who immediately punched several buttons to activate the decoding device.

"Let me get this straight," J. T. said. "You say the fire escape is our best chance?"

Dave Sands nodded. "That's where I used to take my smoke breaks. Nobody ever goes out there."

J. T. nodded and reached into the back of the van, laying hold of a lockbox. Opening it, he pulled out a gleaming automatic weapon and checked the clip. Handing it over to Dave, he produced another, equally effective-looking pistol and tucked it into his waistband. Jake watched in silence as J. T. checked his watch.

"We better get going," J. T. said. "The last shift is due to get off in an hour. That's when we'll make our move."

Jake reached out and grabbed his friend by the arm. "J. T.," he said, choosing his words carefully. "Think about what you're doing. I know you're still upset about Selma . . . and Sherri. But if they were around, I know they wouldn't want you to do this . . . not this way."

J. T. turned to him with a steely look. "And I admired them for that," he replied. "I really did. I know they thought that nonviolence was God's way. And if they were here right now, they'd be doing their best to talk me out of this." He shook his head, pursing his lips. "But they aren't here, are they?" he continued. "And they're not coming back, either. God's will may be different from mine, but we're not living in God's world anymore. We're living in Lucifer's world. And the longer we sit around and do nothing, the longer it's going to be that way."

"But there must be something else we can do," insisted Jake. "There's got to be another way."

J. T. shook his head adamantly. "This is the way, the only way. We've got to do it . . . for all those who no longer can." He turned away from his friend, hiding the tears that had welled up in his eyes.

∽

Judge Wells, still dressed in his black judicial robes, had fallen asleep on the leather couch in his chambers. It had been a long day and in the midst of reviewing a stack of legal briefs, he had passed into a deep and dreamless sleep, undisturbed by compunction for his complicity in the rigged trial or compassion for an innocent woman.

Suddenly the lights over his head came on and in the brightness he sat up, confused and disoriented, to find Victoria Thorne standing over him.

"What are you doing here?" the judge demanded, trying to regain his dignity and rubbing the sleep from his eyes. "Court was over hours ago."

In answer, Victoria held up the small black jamming device that the guards had discovered in Helen's cell a few hours before. "Kendrick has been using this to keep his conversations with Helen Hannah secret," she revealed with an air of outrage. "I just had it checked out in the lab."

Judge Wells smirked, "What's the matter, Counselor?" he asked. "Upset that the opposition is better at dirty tricks than you are?" He stood up, straightening his robes. "I don't know why you're so worried. He may be devious, but he's on our side."

Victoria reached out and boldly grabbed the judge by his arm. Pulling back the black sleeve, she pointed to the mark of 666 on his hand. "Think so?" she asked. "Well, think again. Mitch Kendrick's mark is a fake. And I can prove it."

"Wh-what?" stammered the disbelieving judge. "What are you talking about?"

Victoria nodded grimly. "He's been implanted with a very sophisticated chip. It may fool the detector and he may have even gotten his name on the databank. But you can take my word for it. He's not one of us."

"Who else knows about this?" the judge demanded.

"As of now, just the two of us," the lawyer replied.

Judge Wells breathed a sigh of relief. "Then let's make sure it stays that way," he warned her. "I'd hate to think what Franco Macalousso would do to us if he found out we had an imposter on the team. We've got to get through this trial. Then we can deal with Mitch Kendrick."

"That's an opportunity I'll be looking forward to," Victoria responded ominously.

"The pleasure will be all mine," Judge Wells added with vindictive relish.

Chapter 16

THE DARKNESS OF THE OFFICE was broken by only the faint glint of a streetlight outside the window, shedding its wan light across the carpeted floor and over the figure of a solitary man sitting at a desk, drinking from a glass brimming with hard liquor and staring at a framed photo in his hand.

Mitch Kendrick had been sitting for hours by himself, replaying the events of the day in his mind. He had tried so hard to get Helen to understand what was really important about this trial: not some high ideal or spiritual concept, but the chance to live another day, to see the sun rise one more time, and to take another breath of air.

But she was obsessed with a God who was not only invisible, but completely silent. She wouldn't, or couldn't do what had to be done to save her own life. She was behaving just as his father had and his father had paid the ultimate price.

Mitch looked down again at the picture in his hand. A young boy on a fishing trip with his dad, holding between them the proud catch—a six-pound salmon. Mitch remembered the day vividly and it was one of his most precious memories. He ran his finger absently along a hairline crack in the picture-frame glass as his mind was suddenly flooded with other, agonizing memories.

In his mind's eye he could still see the hard and unforgiving faces of the ONE agents as they burst into the holding cell and grabbed his father by both arms. Their victim didn't struggle. He was ready and willing to meet his fate.

"Dad, please!" Mitch could hear his own words echoing now in his brain. "It's not too late. You still have time. Tell them what they want to hear!"

The voice faded, replaced now by another, calm and certain yet tinged with a deep sadness. "I'm sorry, Son," his father had said over his shoulder as they led him away. "I'm sorry, but I can't do that. I hope that one day you'll understand. Until then, please be strong for me and remember . . . I love you."

It was the last time they had spoken and as Mitch drained his glass of stinging alcohol he could hear himself saying the words he couldn't express that terrible day. "I love you too, Dad," he whispered to himself. "I . . . love you too."

"That's touching," said a voice behind him with a deep growl. "You've got a real sentimental streak, Counselor."

Mitch spun around but before he could see who the intruder was, a pair of strong hands grabbed him and with a single powerful shove, pushed him to the floor and pinned him down.

"I'm sure your dad loved you too," the voice said, and

Mitch could see the dull glint of a knife blade held near his throat. "That is, until they put him out of his misery."

"Who are you?" Mitch cried in a strangled voice. "What do you want?"

"I've got a job to do," the voice replied and Mitch caught a glimpse of an arm draped in dark clothing. He knew immediately that his assailant was the same man who had left the sinister message on his tape recorder, the same man who had been watching him outside his office the night before. "Ms. Thorne is real curious about what you might be cooking up. And she sent me to find out."

Mitch felt the cold touch of steel against his pulsing jugular vein and closed his eyes, waiting for the knife blade to slide deep into his flesh. At that moment the deafening report of a gunshot drove every thought from his mind and he suddenly felt the crushing weight of his assailant as the man collapsed lifelessly on top of him. Breathing heavily from a rush of pure adrenalin, Mitch frantically pushed the corpse off of him and jumped to his feet. Across the dim room, he could see two men, their ONE insignia and the sleek barrels of their guns glinting in the half-light. As he tried desperately to catch his breath, Mitch watched as the lead agent walked up to the dead man, turned over the body with the tip of his steel-toed boot, and knelt down to inspect his kill.

Picking up the corpse's limp hand he studied the mark of 666 with a appraising eye. "These outlaw skin doctors are getting better all the time," he said, looking up at Mitch. "This mark is so good it could have fooled even me."

Mitch nodded, trying to make sense of the flurry of death-dealing events that had just occurred. He felt something wet trickling down his neck and, putting his hand up, found blood oozing from a small knife wound.

"We had a hunch the Haters might try to make contact with you," the agent said. "Since you were defending one of their leaders, we figured they might try and recruit you to their cause." He reached into the breast pocket of his uniform and pulled out the small card Mitch had given Judge Wells earlier with the license number scrawled on the back. "Good thing you were able to report this number," the agent continued. "We were able to trace it down." He looked at the body on the floor. "Looks like we got here just in time."

"But . . . but . . ." stammered Mitch, "why did you have my office under surveillance? I don't understand."

"That's just standard operating procedure in cases like this," replied the agent. "With any trial this high profile, we want to make sure all our bases are covered. We've got plants on each and every player in this game, and we make sure they're following the script down to the last letter."

He signaled to his partner and they both headed for the door. "We'll have a coroner out here in a few hours," he said as they exited. "Meanwhile, try to enjoy the rest of your evening, Counselor." He saluted. "Glory to man."

"Glory to man," Mitch mumbled in response as the door closed and he was left alone to survey the blood and debris that littered his office. Still in a daze, he wandered back to his desk where he again picked up the framed picture of him and his dad on that long-ago fishing expedition. Almost without thinking, he flicked the play button on the tape recorder and, sitting on the floor with his back against the wall, listened as the lonely, forlorn voice of Helen Hannah drifted through the room, a voice captured from the surveillance tape supplied to him by the very ONE who assumed that Mitch was playing for their team.

"Yea, though I walk," she prayed, "through the valley of the shadow of death . . . "

చ్ఛ

The battered van rolled unnoticed through the empty streets surrounding the courthouse and pulled into a parking space directly behind the television news trucks that had gathered to cover the trial of the millennium. Its headlight went out and for a moment there was complete silence before the side door cracked open and slowly slid back. J. T., Jake, and Dave crouched in the shadows in the back of their rolling headquarters. Jake now wore a ONE postal agent uniform that he adjusted nervously while the other two men went through a last-minute check of their equipment, weapons, and building blueprints.

"This is it," J. T. muttered, staring out the open door at the darkened bulk of the courthouse. He turned to Dave Sands. "You're on," he said, clapping him on the shoulder. "We'll wait for our signal."

Dave nodded grimly as he stepped down onto the asphalt of the parking lot.

"God go with you," J. T. whispered behind him.

Dave turned and smiled. "Just remember to save a few chocolate bars for me," he quipped. The van door closed behind him as he made his way across the lot and over the well-tended lawn of the courthouse to a small door on the side of the building, a door almost completely hidden behind a large hedge. As he disappeared around the bush, a ONE patrol car cruised by, its searchlight scanning the perimeter. From their vantage point in the van, Jake and J. T. held their breath until the prowl car turned the corner and disappeared from sight.

Dave, meanwhile, huddled close to the door, his ear against its metal frame, listening for signs of life on the other side. Satisfied that no one would be waiting for him when he opened it, the former ONE security guard inserted a metal–stripped card into the slot at one side of the entrance. Quickly punching up a string of number on the decoder, he watched as the digits on the door's readout aligned themselves one after another. As the final number fell into place there was a soft beeping sound and a click, and the door's lock disengaged. He was in.

Letting out a breath he hadn't realized he'd been holding, Dave slowly opened the door, revealing an empty stairwell. He listened hard. No alarms had been tripped. So far so good. He turned back to the van and waved. It was all systems go.

From across the parking lot, J. T. and Jake exchanged a quick smile. Reaching over to the door handle, J. T. was about to pull it back and spring into action when the night air was rent by the scream of a siren. In the next few seconds events unfolded with blinding speed, yet to the stunned senses of the men, everything was taking place in super-slow motion. From every direction, ONE squad cars seemed to converge out of thin air, their roof lights flashing and the sirens sending up unearthly shrieks. Agents brandishing heavy-duty firepower poured out of the car doors and set off at a dead run across the lot the courthouse lawn.

Still standing in the door, Dave looked for a moment like a deer caught in the headlights of an oncoming eighteen-wheeler. Finally snapping out of his shock, he turned and ran into the building, emerging a moment later pursued by another phalanx of ONE guards. Caught between the two converging ranks, he stopped for a moment and, seeing no way to escape his onrushing doom, pulled a gun from his belt and began firing wildly.

The agents let loose with their own deadly rain of fire and, hit from every direction, Dave dropped to his knees, then fell over onto his face. Weapons still poised, the ONE killers cautiously advanced in a circle around their victim.

"No!" shouted J. T. with a strangled cry as he and Jake watched helplessly from the van. "No!" Scrambling for the door, he lunged for the handle but was blocked by Jake, who knocked him aside and planted himself in his path.

"Don't be stupid, J. T.," he hissed. "What good is it to go out there and get yourself killed along with Dave? Think about it!"

"But we can't just leave him there," J .T. protested, his voice trembling and broken. "You stay. I'll go!"

"No way," objected the tight-lipped Jake. "They get you, they're going to get me for sure. Just sit tight. We've got to survive, J. T. Dave would have wanted it that way."

"But we're the ones that put him up to this," J. T. cried out, then, as the horrifying realization sank in, he whispered, "I'm the one who put him up to this." They turned to watch as the ONE agents moved in closer to Dave's body.

"Check to see if he has any ID," said the lead enforcer.

A second agent moved quickly to comply, kicking the body over with his foot.

In the van, J. T.'s face hardened with hatred. Jake turned to him, knowing the thoughts that were raging through his friend's fevered mind. "He knew the risks, J. T.," Jake reminded him. "You can't blame yourself for what happened."

"It should have been me," J. T. muttered, fingering the trigger guard on the gun in his fist. "It should have been me. Sherri . . . Tony . . . and now Dave. I was the one who was always talking about taking action." He choked back a sob. "And they had to pay the price."

Jake was peering outside as the ONE agents went through their mop-up operation. "There's nothing we can do about it now," he replied. "We're going to have to abort the operation, regroup, and come up with some new options."

J. T. hardly seemed to hear the words. He stared at his boots, the sounds of the gunshots that killed Dave Sands still ringing in his ears. Suddenly a different kind of ring interrupted his desperate thoughts. He reached into a pocket of his tunic and pulled out a cell phone. Hitting the Talk button he identified himself and listened for a long moment. "You . . . what? . . . " he murmured into the line. "But . . . " The phone went dead in his ear. Putting it back in his pocket, he turned again and looked out at the bloody scene in the parking lot. A new determination seemed to dawn in his eyes.

"I'm going in," he said, without turning to Jake.

"What?" demanded the shocked outlaw. "I told you there's no reason to risk your neck now. You'll only add one more body to their count."

"That door is still open," J. T. replied, nodding to the side entrance of the courthouse. "The place is swarming with agents. They're not going to notice one more." He pulled back the safety on his gun. "And God help them if they do."

They both turned to watch as the lawmen began a systematic search of the area around the courthouse. A coroner's truck had arrived and Dave's body was unceremoniously hauled away.

"Think about what you're doing, J. T.," Jake pleaded. "Haven't we lost enough people already?"

J. T. nodded as he reached again for the van door. "That's right," he agreed. "And it's going to stop. As of right now." He jumped from the van and began striding purposefully across the lot toward the blinking lights and milling silhouettes beyond.

"Hey! You," shouted one of the guards as he approached. "Where do you think you're going?"

"Finishing up the security check, sir," came J. T.'s unwavering reply. "Make sure we've cleared the area of cheaters."

The guard nodded. "Proceed," he replied crisply. "And make sure you get copies of all the surveillance tapes from tonight. I'm holding you personally responsible." He squinted in the dim light at J. T.'s face. "What unit are you with again, Sergeant?"

J. T. saluted smartly. "Same as yours, sir," he replied and quickly ducked through the small side door before the curious ONE agent could ask another question. As he entered the building he threw a quick look over his shoulder in the direction of the van, knowing that Jake was watching his every more. There was no turning back now.

∽

By the time the court's heavy oak doors were swung slowly open for the morning session, the stairs and sidewalks outside the building were already clogged with eager onlookers hopeful for a seat on what promised to be the climatic day of the trial. The spectators surged into the hallway leading to Judge Wells's courtroom and it was all the harried guards could do to keep them from storming the doors that led beyond. The camera crews scurried through the press entrance and jockeyed frantically for the best position to view the proceedings.

There was no one in the room who could mistake the electric atmosphere of the court that morning. The scent of blood was in the air. Today was the day Helen Hannah would pay for the consequences of her crimes against One Nation Earth and the reign of the world's beloved messiah, Franco Macalousso.

Fifteen minutes later, after Victoria Thorne, dressed for business in a severe black skirt and jacket, had arrived, the guards escorted the chained defendant to her seat at the defense table among jeers and catcalls. All rose as Judge Wells entered and gaveled the session to order. It was only then that Mitch Kendrick, looking tousled and unshaven, hurried down the aisle and took his place beside his client.

"Glad you could find the time to join us, Counselor," the judge commented in a condescending tone of voice. "I was just beginning to wonder if we'd have to proceed without you."

"I'm sure the prosecution would have applauded that decision," Mitch shot back and caught glares from the judge and Victoria in return.

"Well, then," Wells continued, clearing his throat. "Now that we're all present I assume we can proceed directly to the prosecution's closing statement."

"But, Your Honor," Mitch objected, rising to his feet, "the defense hasn't yet rested its case."

A disquieting murmur ran through the gallery. Victoria and the judge exchanged a petulant look but it was clear that Mitch's legal niceties would have to be observed.

"The defense has another witness?" Judge Wells asked with a sigh.

Beside Mitch at the defense table, Helen smiled.

"Yes, Your Honor," Mitch replied, clearing his throat. He announced loudly, "The defense calls to the stand the chancellor of One Nation Earth: Franco Macalousso."

Chapter 17

A collective gasp of shock rippled through the courtroom at Mitch's surprise announcement. The sound of camera lenses revolving into close-ups of the defense lawyer sounded like the sudden whir of a beehive, while others captured the look of anger and dismay that had transformed the face of Judge Wells into a grim mask.

"Franco Macalousso is a very busy man," he blustered. "I seriously doubt that he's available to respond to every foolish legal maneuver you might want to pull out of your hat, Counselor."

At the table, Helen tugged at her lawyer's sleeve. "What are you doing, Mitch?" she hissed. "This isn't going to help anything."

He leaned down to whisper in her ear. "Leave it to me," he assured her. "This is the way it's got to be." He straightened, addressing the bench again. "Surely," he said, "even Franco Macalousso is not above the law, Your Honor. He says he is a man of the people. This is the people's court. What better place for him to appear?"

"What better place indeed?" said a voice from the back

of the court and a moment later, the TV cameras captured Franco Macalousso himself striding confidently to the witness stand. "I consider it an honor to give my testimony before this court," he continued magnanimously. "After all, my work for the people requires nothing less."

The gallery erupted in cheers at these words, and the judge held back banging his gavel until the tumult subsided on its own accord. There could be no doubt whom the people were rooting for: their leader was among them and their adulation could hardly be contained.

Macalousso took his place at the witness stand and raised his right hand as the courtroom settled into an expectant silence.

"Your Grace," the bailiff began, "there is really no need for you—"

The messiah waved him away with a gesture. "I came into this world to bear witness to the truth," he intoned. "Everyone who loves the truth needs to hear the truth."

More cheers greeted this pronouncement but they quickly dropped off as Judge Wells turned to Mitch. "You may proceed then, Counselor," he instructed.

Taking a deep breath, the lawyer moved closer to the charismatic world leader. "Thank you, Your Eminence," he said, smiling at Macalousso, then leaned closer over the witness stand railing. "Perhaps," he continued, "you could tell why, in your opinion, we are here in this courtroom today."

"Of course," replied Macalousso smoothly. "We're here because your client," he pointed to Helen, "this poor individual refuses to see the truth that has been laid out before her and before all mankind. She still insists on blindly obeying her fears and prejudices."

He had fixed Helen with a malevolent stare as he spoke and she felt a cold chill race down her spine as he continued.

"She chooses to condemn the work I have done on behalf of suffering humanity. She pretends that a world exists beyond this present reality, a world that is more important than the one we are living in today."

Helen threw a pleading glance to her lawyer. Why was he letting this travesty continue? "But the real reason we are having this trial," Macalousso concluded, "is because Helen Hannah clings to her dangerous and destructive belief in an ancient lie—a lie called Jesus Christ."

Unable to stand another word, Helen jumped to her feet. "How dare you?" she shouted. "It's you who are a liar! It's you who are the father of lies!"

"Silence!" shouted Judge Wells, bringing down his gavel with a thunderous crack. "Silence, or I will have you removed from this courtroom immediately."

Mitch stepped forward. "Don't blame her, Your Honor. Even our esteemed witness here has called my client a poor and deluded specimen of humanity. She can't be held to fault. It's what—who—she believes that is to blame."

Helen looked at him furiously. "No, Mitch!" she blurted out, shaking her head. "That's not true and you know it! Why are you doing this?"

"She'd be a decent, law-abiding, and productive member

of society if it were not for the one she calls her God," the attorney continued relentlessly.

"Stop!" screamed Helen. "He doesn't represent me! I demand a new lawyer. This man is trying to convict me!"

"Enough!' Judge Wells thundered and turning to the guards, commanded, "Remove the defendant immediately. I will not have my courtroom made a mockery of."

The crowd jeered, hurling insults as Helen was dragged away, but the prisoner didn't seem to hear. Instead, she focused intently on her lawyer, trying to capture his eyes with her own and seek out the answer to the agonizing question: why?

"Mitch! Please!" she cried, but he wouldn't look her way, deliberately turning his head the other direction as she passed amidst the tumult of the raucous gallery.

"Does the defense wish to rest?" Judge Wells asked smugly as order was restored.

Mitch took a deep breath, trying to clear his head of the image of his client being dragged away like a rabid animal, and turned to the bench. "A few more questions, Your Honor," he requested.

"As you wish, Counselor," replied Judge Wells, beaming solicitously at Macalousso.

Mitch moved back toward his witness. "Your Eminence," he began, "to those of us gathered in this courtroom today, it may well be obvious why Helen Hannah should accept that you are who you say you are—the true savior of the world. But for the benefit of the record, could you please explain it once again?"

"Of course," Macalousso replied. "All you need do is look around you. The miracles I have performed. The healings I have accomplished. The peace and prosperity I have brought to mankind. I have made this world on heaven on earth."

In response to his words, the crowd broke into cheers of unabashed adoration, joining together to chant the name of their messiah until the walls of the courtroom shook.

ฟ๛

The door to the holding cell slammed open and Helen was hurled to the floor by her burly guards with a brutality that mirrored the contempt they felt for their prisoner. She lay still for a moment, tasting blood from a split lip sustained in her fall, and listened as a loudspeaker mounted in the cell broadcasted the proceedings from the courtroom.

Suddenly she felt a pair of hands on her body, hands far different from those that had sent her hurling to the concrete floor. The kind and loving caresses caused her to look up and into the face of Selma Davis, also being held in the cell to await her fate. The two women hugged, their tears mingling as they shared both the joy of reunion and the sorrow of their circumstances.

ฟ๛

"I'd like to ask the court's indulgence to perform a simple demonstration, Your Honor," Mitch said as the two women listened intently.

"What is the nature of this demonstration?" asked Judge Wells dubiously, then looked to Franco Macalousso, still seated in the witness stand, for a clue as to how he should proceed.

"It will take only a moment of the court's time and is vital to my case," answered Mitch and from the stand, Macalousso nodded permission to the judge.

"Proceed, Counselor," ordered the judge.

Crossing to the defense table, Mitch opened his brief-case and produced a revolver. Cries of consternation were heard in the gallery and several of the guards stationed around the room began to move toward him.

Mitch held up his hands to calm the crowd. "There's no need to worry," he quickly explained. "I intend to remove all the bullets in front of you all." He looked to the judge. "May I, Your Honor?"

The judge, with a nervous glimmer in his eye, nodded. He wasn't sure he liked where this was going.

Opening the chamber of the revolver, Mitch dropped the bullets into the palm of his hand and closed the cylinder with a snap. Crossing to the bailiff, he pressed the bullets into his hand. "Please keep these safe for me," he requested and, still holding the gun, moved back toward the center of the courtroom.

Mitch looked around the room and into the packed gallery, seeming to make eye contact with each and every person there. After a long moment, he cleared his throat and began to speak, his voice ringing through the marble halls of justice. "With so very many passionate followers of our esteemed witness here today," he began, "I wonder how many among you would be ready to express your total and complete commitment to this man and his mission." He pointed to Macalousso as the crowd once again erupted in cheers, their hands raised as if asking to be chosen to show their love and loyalty.

"Excellent," Mitch continued. "With such an outpouring it should be no problem to find one among you all," he spread his arms wide, the pistol still in one hand, "just one who would be willing to participate in my demonstration."

More shouts and cries met his words and Mitch turned back to the judge. "Your Honor, given this enthusiastic response, I would like to call to the stand my final witness." His voice rose. "I call anyone who is willing to lay down his life for Franco Macalousso!"

This time, a confused silence was the only response.

"Come, come, ladies and gentlemen," Mitch cajoled. "I call anyone, anyone at all, willing to give up his life in exchange for Lucifer's." As he spoke the name, Mitch lifted the pistol and pointed it directly at Macalousso's head.

The gasps and cries of alarm from the crowd mingled with barked orders of the ONE agents for the courtroom guards to level their weapons at the lawyer. For a moment pandemonium reigned as Macalousso, unfazed, watched the chaos around him, a slight ironic smile playing on his lips.

"Count the bullets, please," Mitch said to the bailiff, his voice clearly heard above the angry and frightened crowd.

Silence fell as the bailiff obeyed, dropping the bullets

one at a time from his right hand to his left. "F-five," he stammered at last, his voice catching on the word.

A shock wave of horror spread through the courtroom at the news.

"Five," Mitch repeated, "which means that one remains in the chamber of this gun." He looked at the crowd again without taking the gun from Macalousso's temple. "Let me ask again," he repeated. "Who among all of you loyal followers of your messiah will step forward to take a bullet in his place?"

The silence grew ever more deafening. The crowd members looked at one another, then turned away in shame and embarrassment, hanging their heads. The self-satisfied smile on their savior's face began to dissolve into a look of anger and hate.

∽

In the holding cell, Helen and Selma listened with disbelief and growing sense of triumph as the stillness in the court-room stretched through long minutes. Mitch's bold strategy was beginning to come clear and for the first time since their ordeal began, both women felt the faint stirrings of hope.

The sound of approaching footsteps caused the agents standing guard to shift nervously and finger the handles of the guns in their holsters. The door suddenly opened and a man stepped inside. The eyes of both Helen and Selma widened, but a quick look from J. T. was enough to warn them not to reveal his identity.

Saluting the guards, J. T. pulled a fabricated ID from his uniform pocket and flashed it. "Report to the court at once," he ordered them. "We've got a situation." The guards hesitated, looking at each other and back to J. T. "Do I look like a patient man to you?" he snapped, then added, "I wouldn't suggest waiting around to find out."

The guards hustled out of the office and J. T. threw the two women a wink and a broad smile.

⧼⧽

The silence in the courtroom was like a thick fog, enveloping everything. Mitch stood frozen in place, still pointing the gun directly at Macalousso, whose face was now dark with rage. Then, without warning, he swung the weapon over and aimed it at Victoria Thorne.

"How about you, Ms. Prosecutor?" he asked. "Won't you step forward to save your messiah?" Victoria's face drained of all color, leaving only her flashing eyes to convey the loathing and homicidal impulses she was feeling toward the defense attorney.

Mitch stepped closer, a light of vindication burning in his eyes, the gun pointed at a spot at the exact middle of her forehead. "Come on, Vicky," he urged. "Don't you want to go down in history for saving the savior of mankind?"

The hatred on Victoria's face now turned to fear as the

muzzle of the gun came ever closer. She shook her head and looked away, mortified by her behavior and what it said about the claims she had been making all along for Franco Macalousso.

At last, Mitch stood directly in front of the prosecution table, where he gently set down the gun and turned back to face the bench. A audible sigh of relief could be heard throughout the courtroom.

"I don't blame you, Ms. Prosecutor," he continued softly, and then turned to the gallery. "I don't blame any of you. Death is a sobering reality when it's staring you in the face. And to die for someone else—well, as I once read in a book somewhere, there is no greater sacrifice."

∽

The words rang out loud and clear over the holding-cell speakers as J. T. ransacked a small desk at the guard station until he found a ring of keys in a bottom drawer.

"Hurry, J. T.," Selma urged him as he tried each key in the door lock, muttering in frustration after each failed attempt. At last, a key produced a telltale click of opening tumblers and, with a powerful shove, he pushed against the heavy metal door. It refused to move and, with mounting anxiety, he jiggled the key in the lock. It was stuck. "This can't be happening," he said in bitter disbelief and turned to look at the two women staring wide-eyed at him. "This can't be happening," he repeated as they rushed up and began frantically pushing at the jammed door. Outside, down the hall, the sound of rapidly approaching footsteps could suddenly be heard.

∾

Every eye in the courtroom was now turned to the bench, where Judge Wells, as he had done throughout the trial, could be expected to restore order and decorum. After all, everyone knew how this trial was supposed to end. How could the judge let things slip away like this? "What exactly is the point of this little display?" Wells demanded, his jowls trembling as he glared down at Mitch.

"Simple, Your Honor," replied the lawyer. "Franco Macalousso here has offered the human race heaven on earth. We heard him say so here today. But, as we have all admitted so graphically today, this body, like this whole earth, will one day pass away. And when that happens, life as we know it comes to a sudden and final end."

"Be careful, Counselor," the judge warned darkly. "You are dangerously close to contempt with such statements."

"The truth can't be hidden, Your Honor," Mitch insisted, turning to the bank of television cameras. "The truth is, God conquered death through His unconditional love for His creatures. For each and every one of us. That is why Christians will always renounces false saviors such as Franco Macalousso. Because the truth can't be denied!"

The gallery, shaken from its long silence, burst into a clamor of outraged indignation. Shouts were heard for Mitch to be arrested, taken away, and worse. The entire courtroom threatened to become a slaughterhouse at any moment.

From the witness stand, Franco Macalousso, discarding the last of his serene detachment, rose and thundered at the defense attorney. "Kendrick!" he wailed. "This very day you shall know that I and I alone am the king and ruler of this world! Not your so-called God. Not His Son, Jesus Christ!"

In answer, Mitch raised his arm and in the air and with the finger of his other hand, ripped off the mark of 666 from his skin.

The shouts became shrieks of pure demonic frenzy, with the voice of Victoria rising above the rest.

"My treasure lies in heaven!" Mitch shouted above the fray. "This world will pass away and all its treasures with it! I renounce the mark of the beast, I denounce this false trial and the lies that it has spread!"

His words triggered a outbreak of mass hysteria. As Judge Wells banged the gavel helplessly, the crowd rushed down from the gallery, pouring into the aisles, and the ONE guards tried desperately to stem the swirling flow of enraged humanity. Several grabbed Mitch and tried to pull him out a side exit, fighting with the crowd every step of the way. Behind the relative security of the roped-off media section, the TV cameras captured the entire chaotic spectacle and beamed it simultaneously to the far corners of the earth.

ᴕ

The pounding of approaching boots seemed to send tremors through the holding cell, each footfall another point on the Richter scale. The door remained jammed and J. T., Helen, and Selma had stepped back from it, sore and out of breath from their efforts to open it. With a determined look, J. T. pulled the gun he was carrying from its holster and checked the lock and load mechanisms.

"No, J. T.!" Selma shouted. "This can't be the way!" She turned to Helen. "Pray! Pray now!"

J. T., his adrenalin pumping wildly, looked from the two praying women to the door and back again. The struggle over the choice he had to make was clearly written on his face. At that moment the door burst open from the outside and a squad of ONE guards rushed in to the women, guns drawn.

"You!" shouted the lead guard to J. T. "Let's see some ID. Pronto!"

J. T., the gun hidden behind his back, felt for the trigger with his forefinger. Behind him he could hear Selma whispering urgently to him. "Please don't," she pleaded. "Think, J. T., how Jesus has shown us a different way, a better way. Think what Sherri would want you to do."

Her words began to sink in and, his face very pale and his lips drawn in a tight line, J. T. slipped the weapon under his belt behind his back and slowly began to raise his hands. Over the intercom, the turmoil in the courtroom had reached a new level of intensity and was suddenly interrupted by an tense announcement.

"All available personnel to the courtroom," the voice on the speaker commanded. "All available personnel to the courtroom! Immediately!"

Without a second thought the squad of guards turned and rushed from the holding cell. For a long moment J. T. and the women stood motionless, holding their breath as if waiting for permission to breathe. A barely audible click was heard and, as if by some invisible hand, the door swung open.

"Saved by a voice from above," Helen remarked with a broad grin and the three made their escape down the hallway.

∽

In the confusion and bedlam of the courtroom, the judge's gavel sounded small and insignificant. Mitch, surrounded by guards, was being protected long enough for them to slip a pair of handcuffs over his wrist. The charges would come later: disturbing the peace, contempt of court, enemy of One Nation Earth, and blasphemer against the messiah, Franco Macalousso.

But for Victoria Thorne, the wheels of justice turned far too slowly and her thirst for vengeance burned deep inside. Grabbing the gun from the prosecution table, she moved stealthily through the milling mob, coming up to Mitch and the guards around him from behind. When they saw who was approaching, the uniformed men fell back, intimidated by the look of sheer determination on her face and the raised gun pointed at Mitch's chest.

"You think you've won?" she asked with sneering contempt. "You've won nothing. The victory is mine and always has been. I will be called a heroine for what I'm about to do. And your name will forever go down in infamy."

The report of a gunshot was heard echoing through the courtroom and brought the rampaging crowd to a sudden and silent halt. They backed away, making a circle around Victoria and the crumpled figure of Mitch, bleeding from a chest wound.

Bending down, Victoria whispered a last derisive message into the dying man's ear. "You're a fool," she told him. "A fool . . . just like your old man."

Mitch looked up at her through clouded eyes, his lids fluttering as his life ebbed away. A smile, peaceful and beatific, spread over his face, as if a beautiful vision had suddenly appeared before him. With a shudder and a sigh he took a final, ragged breath and lay still, the smile still lingering on his features. The camera moved in closer, capturing his expression for the whole world to see.

Among those watching the haunting image was a tearful young woman, sitting in the corner of the shabby lobby of a tenement hotel in a bad downtown neighborhood. As the image of Mitch's face hung frozen on the TV screen in the lobby, Dawn bowed her head, clasping her hands together, and began to pray as around her the dazed and drunken old men continued to stare at the flickering picture.

The silence in the courtroom was conveyed through the holding-cell floor by the intercom speakers as J. T., Helen, and Selma made their way swiftly down the long hallway. Turning a corner, J. T. took a quick look in both directions. "It's clear," he told his companions and pointed to a corridor leading to the left. "We'll take this way. I'm pretty sure it leads to the street."

Helen held out her hand to stop him. "But what about Mitch?" she asked. "We can't leave him behind."

J. T. held her by her shoulders. "Listen to me, Helen," he said, his voice racing against time. "This is the way Mitch planned it. Don't you see? He wanted you out of the courtroom. That's why he was baiting you—making you angry, getting you to react. He wanted to make sure you were safely out of the way before he . . . did what he had to do."

"But," Helen began, choking back a sob. "How? Why? He was on our side! What brought him over? What changed his mind?"

"I don't think it was his mind so much as his heart," remarked J. T., a light of compassion and understanding burning in his eyes. "But when we had a chance to be alone for a moment before all this went down, he asked me to tell you something."

"What?' Helen asked, her own eyes brimming with tears.

"Remember when you thought you were alone, praying?" J. T. asked. "Macalousso's men were listening. But they weren't the only ones. Mitch Kendrick heard your prayers too. He wanted you to know that. He wanted you to know that prayers can be answered, even when we're not sure we even believe that anyone's listening." He held her close as she began to weep and, after a moment, led her down the hall and through a door that led into the dark night and freedom.

༺༻

Franco Macalousso sat impassively at his large desk, the panorama of the city skyline spread out behind him through a picture window. In his hands he held a newspaper, but his eyes were not on the screaming headline. Instead he fixed a steely and unforgiving gaze at the two people who stood contritely before him.

"Well, Ms. Thorne and Judge Wells," he began in a soft and sinister voice. "It seems we all meet again." He tapped the newspaper in his hand. "Sadly it is not under the happiest of circumstances. You know," he continued, stroking his chin, "they say there is no such thing as bad publicity. They also say there's no such thing as hell. Well," he concluded, his eyes glowing red in the half-light of the room, "I think you two are about to discover just how wrong they can be."

He pushed a button on his desk and several heavy-set guards suddenly appeared. As he watched them take away the new prisoners, Franco Macalousso hardly noticed the newspaper lying face up on his desk.

"Mistrial!" the headline announced and beneath it, the boldface words: "Case Against God Dropped. Helen Hannah Escapes."

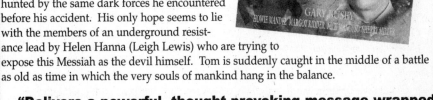

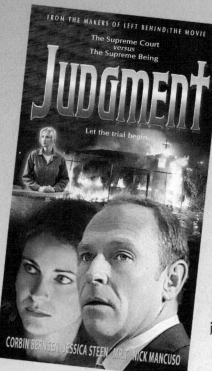

Based on the Runaway Bestseller

On an overseas flight to London, journalist Buck Williams (Kirk Cameron) and pilot Rayford Steele (Brad Johnson) are caught in the middle of the most incredible event in history. Suddenly, without warning, dozens of passengers simply vanish into thin air. But it doesn't stop there. It soon becomes clear that millions of people are missing from around the world.

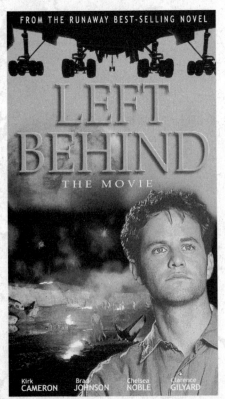

As chaos and anarchy engulf the world, both men set out on vastly different paths in a desperate search for answers.

Filled with suspense, action and adventure, and based on the *New York Times* bestselling novel by Tim LaHaye and Jerry B. Jenkins, this riveting motion picture will take you on a spellbinding journey through the most mysterious book of the Bible—the book of Revelation.

Available at your favorite bookstore.